BEYOND
DECEIT

A. MORIEL MCCLERKLIN

ISBN 10: 0692917950
ISBN 13: 9780692917954

ACKNOWLEDGMENT

Thanks to my family, the elders, and all those who encouraged me to manifest the best that's in me.

Love recognizes no barriers. It jumps hurdles, leaps fences, penetrates walls to arrive at its destination full of hope.

—Maya Angelou

PART ONE

CHAPTER 1

As on most mornings in the spring, Solomon woke as the first sunlight touched his face. Opening his eyes, he gazed upon the blue waters of Lake Michigan. This view of the lake was one of the joys of living on the forty-eighth floor of a condominium next to Navy Pier. On a clear sunny morning like this one, the lakefront view was breathtaking.

He grabbed his robe and strolled out to the balcony to immerse in the cool breeze and the sun's ascent into an orange sky. Joggers and bikers had already started lining the trail that ran along the shoreline, and a few adventurous sailors had hoisted their sails and steered into the blue distance. He could hear the noise of waves kissing the shore and the shrill of pelicans—nature's soundtrack for his morning.

Except on cold days, the balcony was his sacred space, the place where he went to quiet his mind and commune with his deeper self. He sat back on his balcony chair and bathed in the warmth of the sun's radiance. He then began his ritual for settling into a state of serenity. Closing his eyes, he took in a breath of air and exhaled slowly, repeating the exercise a few times.

Each morning for the past few weeks, he'd made this trip to his balcony, trying to deal with the disturbance within his soul—the constant pull of worries and anxieties that gained a stronger grip each day. However, today, like the day before it, the inner peace he sought eluded him.

He stood and leaned over the edge of the balcony. Staring out, he reflected upon the shifts he allowed to occur within his character over the past three years. He'd acted in ways that violated his inner covenant and had made choices that were not aligned with the values he'd held. Those choices and actions now threatened the stability of the successful world he'd built.

He inhaled another deep breath and exhaled slowly. He now realized that his predicament couldn't end unless he faced it and finally did what he should've done a long time ago.

Suddenly, the sound of Jan, his wife, busying about the house caught his attention and diverted his thoughts from the clouds overhead and the storm that was at hand. She was already up preparing the things he needed for his monthly trip to Washington, DC. As a senior executive in an information-technology firm headquartered in Chicago, he traveled to DC each month to provide consultant services for a client of his company. These monthly trips had been his routine for the past three years.

Her entrance onto the balcony signaled an end to his attempts to grapple with the worries of the moment.

"You better get moving if you're going to catch your plane on time," she said, grabbing his butt. He managed a laugh to conceal his anguish.

"Stop that before I call the police and have you charged with sexual abuse," he jested, turning and looking back at her.

"Who, me?" She smirked as she squeezed him again.

"Yes, you," he responded, turning around, pulling her close and kissing her. She meant the world to him, and for the first time in his life, he feared losing her.

"You're going to need to start getting ready to go, soon."

"I know."

"Do you think anyone will ever take your place on this assignment? By now, shouldn't you have your work in DC at a place where it can easily be handed off to someone else on the team?"

Lately, she'd been growing less excited about the idea of him taking the assignment. He knew that while she understood it would help him scale the corporate ladder, the thought of him being away from her for a week each month stirred insecurities within her. They'd never spent that amount of time apart from each other before, and, although she'd grown more comfortable with the routine, recently, she'd expressed that she wished the assignment would end soon.

"I'm not trying to pressure you. You know I support whatever you have to do for the company and your career, but honestly, I look forward to the day when I won't have to be away from my man five days each month."

"You know I understand, Jan. This monthly travel wears on me too, but I can't say how much longer I'll be doing this."

Like her, he also wished he could end this three-year stint. More than that, he wished he'd never started making these trips to Washington. He wouldn't be facing the troubles that beset him now if he'd simply refused his boss's request. For the company, it was a good decision; however, for his personal life, he now regretted it.

"Do you have everything packed for me?"

"Everything is packed and ready, sir." She smiled and made a salute. "Why are you asking me that in the first place? Have you ever known me to drop the ball when preparing for your travel?"

"You're right. You've always been the woman I could count on."

He cupped her face tenderly in his hands and pulled her lips to meet his. Then he rested his face against hers and held her, as his body trembled from the worries that plagued him.

"Is everything okay?" she asked, pulling back from him.

Her question added to the anxieties he was already feeling. He knew he had to be careful. The last thing he needed was for her to become suspicious and start an investigation into his miseries. She was like Perry Mason when it came to interrogating anyone about anything.

"Yes," he said as he tried to get a grip on himself. "Your question about how much longer this assignment will last made me realize how much I'm also tired of being away from you."

She smiled in a way that said she was pleased to hear that they were both on the same page about his trips.

"Go on and get ready so you can get out of here," she said, still smiling.

At her command, he jumped into the shower, got dressed, and went into the dining room, where she'd prepared his favorite traveling breakfast: a glass of apple juice, one egg sunny-side up, wheat toast with orange preserves, and a bowl of sliced strawberries. He sat down to the table; however, his appetite wasn't there. She sat across from him watching as he moved the food around with his fork while not really eating anything.

"You sure you're all right? It seems like something's troubling you."

"Yes, I'm fine. It's just that now you've got me feeling like I really don't want to go anywhere."

"I'm sorry, baby. Please don't feel that way," she said, placing her hand on his. "We both can endure this temporary separation a bit longer."

The touch of her hand was comforting.

"You're right; it will all work out," he said, feeling a little more confident.

Feeling the time passing, he looked at his watch. Realizing it was time for him to leave for the airport, he pushed the plate to the side, with his food mostly untouched. He rose, gave her another kiss, thanked her one more time, and walked out the door, heading downstairs to the sedan waiting to take him to Midway for his morning flight. It was a journey into another town, another life, and the eye of his storm.

CHAPTER 2

After lying back down for an hour once Solomon had left, Jan got up and busied herself about the condo, trying to tidy the place before she headed out to work. Cleanliness was a habit she'd learned from her mother. Never wanting to leave the place untidy, she hurried to get things in order. Although she always went to work in the late morning on the days that Solomon traveled to Washington, traffic to Rosemont would still be heavy. Therefore, she'd soon need to walk out the door.

After ensuring the rest of the house was neat, she made her way to Solomon's closet. It was always her last cleaning stop. As she began to arrange things, she noticed that one of his blazers had fallen off its hanger. Reaching down to pick it up, she saw a receipt inside his pocket. Knowing that he sometimes left important business receipts inside his jackets, she reached inside the pocket to retrieve it and noticed that it was from a dinner cruise for two on the Potomac.

I don't remember Solomon telling me about a dinner cruise.

The receipt sparked a concern.

Is this a business or personal receipt? Regardless, why didn't he mention the cruise to me?

The thought of Solomon keeping secrets from her was troubling. In the past, he'd never kept anything from her. Instead, he'd always been honest, and that was a big part of what she loved about him. Still, here was a receipt for a cruise he'd failed to mention. Questions began to crowd her mind, triggering suppressed insecurities.

Having tragically lost her father, the first man she loved, she struggled with attachment issues—namely, a deep phobia of losing any man she'd come to cherish. Her father had died from injuries sustained in the Vietnam War when she was young, leaving her mother—Beatrice—and her younger brother and sister to face the world of Milwaukee, Wisconsin, alone. His death left emotional scars for everyone in the family, particularly for her. She was the firstborn and the girl he desperately wanted, which had given her a special place in his heart as *daddy's girl*—a space she adored occupying. He'd spent a lot of time with them, taking them on outings to parks, the zoo, and other interesting places. Thus, while her brother and sister were too young when he died to remember much about him, she held vivid and fond memories of him and their times together—a fact that made his death even more painful to her.

Her father's death caused her to develop trepidations about investing her heart in a relationship, fearing the possibility of losing a man she loved again. Consequently, she became cautious and deliberate about finding someone who could fulfill her need for commitment and security. Solomon had proven to be the right choice. He was trusting and faithful, which helped her to overcome her fear of forming a close bond with someone. It was the main reason she'd chosen him from among other suitors.

However, his three years of travel had caused her insecurities to resurface. She began to worry about whether he would maintain his faithfulness to their marriage being away from her like that each month. Thus, she started longing for his monthly sojourns to soon end.

Given her insecurities about his monthly trips, even with no evidence that she should be concerned about his time away from her, she knew that any tangible reasons for suspicion could push her over the edge of worry. Now here was a receipt for a dinner cruise that he'd failed to mention. She could feel the distrust trying to form in her mind, but she knew it was dangerous to allow her thoughts to wander into such a place. She understood that any seeds of misgiving about his fidelity that she allowed to be sown into her thoughts would easily blossom into the phobia she'd struggled to overcome.

Determined to prevent any thoughts of suspicion from gaining a stronghold in her mind, she decided to let her worries sparked by the receipt go.

I've never had a reason to distrust him in the past and there's no need to start now. I'll simply ask him about the receipt when I talk to him. I'm sure that he can explain it.

She was committed to moving on with her day; however, upon her first chance to talk with him, she definitely wanted answers.

CHAPTER 3

Jan knew she should've been on her way out the door to work by now. An hour had passed, and still she couldn't shake the unsettling feeling that finding the receipt caused her. She'd thought it would be easy to put the suspicions out of her mind until she'd had the chance to talk to Solomon, but it wasn't. In a dark crevice of her thoughts, the unthinkable had started to form, and she found its nagging accusation hard to resist.

One week per month for three years was a lot of time alone from me. Any man would be tempted to fill that space, the voice in her mind reasoned.

But he's different, she argued back. *The man he is would never compromise himself, let alone our marriage.*

It was a good rebuttal, but the indictment against him continued in her head.

Yes, he's a man of strong convictions, but he's still a man, and as such, he's capable of yielding to temptations in a vulnerable moment.

Feeling the tremors in her body, she grabbed a wine bottle from the rack, poured a small amount in a glass, and drank it. She'd never in the past taken a drink before going to work, but she had to do something to calm herself. Afterward, she tried to put on her makeup, but her shaking hands made it difficult.

Realizing that she was losing the argument for trusting him, she tried to settle her mind by focusing on the things she absolutely knew to be true about him. She could hardly imagine the Solomon she'd known and loved since college engaging in some deceitful activity. Staring at her favorite picture of them together, she thought back to the start of their relationship.

―――――

They both had attended Bradley University. She was a psychology major, and he was studying management information systems. They were both in their second semester and shared a literature class. She was very interested in the way he viewed literature, as he seemed to love words as she did. Thus, at the end of one of their class sessions, she suggested that they meet at the student center later and discuss their common passion for literary expressions. This began their ritual of spending time together.

As they engaged in moments of literary discussions, she found their intellectual intercourse stimulating. It amused her that their minds were so much alike even though they often ended up on opposite sides of an issue.

Their interactions enhanced her comprehension of him. He was open and transparent about himself, which made him unique among the young men she'd known prior to him. She'd always felt that they had hidden motives—namely, to get inside her panties. Yet Solomon seemed to truly value the woman she was on the inside. Thus, she reciprocated his transparency by opening to him a window into her mind and through her mind into her soul. The view for both of them was captivating.

The more they engaged each other in talk, the more she could feel the emotional connection between them getting stronger. She was developing an interest in him, and she could see a corresponding affection in his eyes. After their first kiss, she asked him where he saw their romance going. "I need you," he answered, with a depth of feeling that lowered all her emotional defenses. Letting her guard down, she unlocked the doorway to her heart, and he entered in gladly. Once he was inside, she knew it was a space he'd been born to occupy.

She was still a virgin when she met him. Although initially he made a few attempts at seducing her, she admonished him saying she wasn't ready for lovemaking and that they should take their time and not be in a hurry. She explained that she couldn't give herself that way without a long-term commitment.

"You can say I'm old fashioned in that sense," she'd told him. "I don't think I could ever make love to a man without being married to him."

He understood and never pressed her again about sex, but then that *magical* night happened!

It was June, and their junior year at Bradley had just ended. The night was beautiful as a full strawberry moon with its yellow tint filled the sky. To release the stress from a challenging school year, they went to see the production of *For Colored Girls Who Have Considered Suicide* at the Goodman Theatre.

Like the audience, she was engrossed in the two-hour performance. The play was about seven women dressed in different colors, fading in and out of the light while revealing the physical, mental, and emotional scars that resulted from dealing with a hostile society and their black male lovers. Midway through the play, she began to cry. After the Lady in Red finished her gripping poetic climax—revealing how her man, Willie Brown, dropped their two children from their fifth-floor window—she was emotionally consumed.

When the play ended, she and Solomon headed back to his uncle's apartment in Hyde Park. His uncle stayed on the road for extended periods, driving trucks for a national moving company, and he allowed Solomon to stay at the apartment during summer breaks as a way of keeping him from returning to the old West Side neighborhoods and the dangers it held for young black men.

When they arrived, Solomon poured her and himself a glass of wine, and they began the analysis that followed any event they attended.

"It was the most painful depiction of black women's lives that I've ever witnessed," he said. "It certainly made me more sensitive to the abuses that they've experienced."

"You're right," she said. "Black women have lived through much harshness, and the play was a harrowing testimony to that fact. In truth Solomon, listening to the women in the play describe their heartbreaking experiences with men reaffirmed how blessed I am to have a man like you—loving me completely, giving so much of yourself, respecting me highly, and caring so much. It's not that I took our relationship for granted; it's just that the play awakened me to a more appreciable clarity of our love. I'm grateful for you."

She leaned over and held him as her eyes began to moisten. He grabbed her face and started kissing her tears and then her lips. As he held her affectionately, the touch of his hands aroused her. With her passions inflamed, she took his hand and placed it under her dress while they continued to kiss lovingly.

He appeared nervous as he touched her gently with his fingers, a new but pleasing experience that caused her such delight. As they continued, she pulled off her underwear and then took off her dress and bra.

"Are you sure?" he whimpered as she unveiled herself to him for the very first time.

"In all this time of waiting, I've never been as sure of anything as I am now," she whispered in his ear.

Aroused by the sensual journey they were now taking, he stripped himself, climbed atop her, and crossed the threshold into her intimate region. Releasing pent-up feelings, they groaned and moaned as their bodies gyrated together in lustful passions. The wetness of their kisses, the sweat from their bodies' embrace, and the flow of sacred waters were intoxicating.

Reveling in the pleasures of the moment, she celebrated all that was now good in her life. She sighed and said to him in a low voice, "I'll only give myself to one man, and that man is you."

He vowed back in a whisper, "I'll always be yours."

With the union of their souls consummated, they continued to drink from the cup of indulgence, relishing every second of intimate bliss.

The next morning, he grabbed her, jumped into his car, and drove to Wisconsin to get Beatrice's permission to marry her. Beatrice consented but required them both to finish school first. A year later, they attended graduation in the morning and got married in the evening. Although they wanted children, she experienced complications that would keep them from fulfilling that desire.

———

Leaving her precious thoughts of the past, with her concerns about the receipt still tormenting her, she returned to his closet and started searching through all of his pockets to see what else she could find. She was relieved that the search came up empty, and she began to feel embarrassed about the way she was feeling.

Why did I let that receipt create this much suspicion in my mind?

Considering the emotional challenge she was now experiencing, she recognized that she'd need extra time to get to work this morning. Therefore, she grabbed her phone and called her office. When the receptionist answered, she instructed her to pass on to the appropriate people that something came up but that she'd definitely be in the office later.

Following her call to work, she walked back into the bedroom and sat down on the bed. She wished she could call him, hear him explain everything to her, as she was certain he would, and thereby overcome this dreadful emotional pull she was now fighting. Assuring herself that she was overreacting to the discovery of the receipt and cruise, she lay down and drifted off to sleep.

PART TWO

Three years earlier.

CHAPTER 4

Solomon had been making these trips to DC for the past nine months. It was the end of his third day in town, and he'd decided to break from his normal after-work routine of returning to the hotel, eating dinner, heading to his room, talking to Jan, and going to sleep. Instead, he'd go to a nearby sports bar, do some drinking, and watch the Bulls-Wizards basketball game.

He took a seat near the end of the bar and started looking at the menu. Afterward, he motioned for the bartender and then ordered food and something to drink. After he'd consumed his second glass of wine, she walked in and sat on the stool at the end of the bar, next to his. She was tall and slim but nicely shaped. Most of all, she was attractive.

He could tell she was the friendly type who enjoyed being around others from the smile she beamed as she entered the room. Her eyes and smile seemed to invite people in. Although he tried not to pay attention to her, there was something familiar about her, but he couldn't put his finger on what it was. Despite his pretending not to notice her, she looked over at him and started talking.

"Hi, my name is Evelyn. What are you drinking? Let me buy you another round."

He turned away from the game toward her. Gazing directly at her reinforced his sense that they had met somewhere before tonight. *Where?* he wondered. He struggled to pull the answer from his memory, but without success.

Reacting to the delay in his response, she said to the bartender, "Give him another of whatever he's drinking, on me."

Hearing her directive to the bartender, he snapped out of his memory scan. He wasn't accustomed to women being that forward with him, but even more, something about her stirred uneasiness within him.

"Thanks for the offer, but I'm good for now. I've had two drinks already," he said and returned to watching the game.

Glancing back over at her, he noticed that she seemed a little embarrassed by his rejection of her offer. Then he saw her looking down at his wedding ring.

Now that she sees I'm married, maybe she'll back off from trying to talk to me, he thought. However, he was wrong.

"What's the matter?" she started back up, apparently undeterred by seeing his ring. "You aren't the sociable type? When I'm out at a bar, I like to get to know people, particularly the person sitting next to me. Since that happens to be you, you're obligated to be my chatting partner tonight," she said with a grin. "But if you're not in the talking mood, you can change seats, and I'll just talk to that man sitting on the other side of you. Sir," she said to the person sitting to Solomon's right, "do you mind talking to a beautiful woman while you drink and watch the game?"

"Not at all," the man answered enthusiastically.

While Solomon wasn't necessarily excited about the idea of talking with her, he did think that it might help him remember where he may have met her.

"It's not necessary for us to change seats," he said, loosening his guard. "Forgive me for being a little reserved. I'm not from here; I'm from Chi-town. My mother always cautioned me to be careful talking to strangers," he said in jest.

She laughed. "You're worried that I might kidnap you and take you off somewhere? I've certainly been known to do that to handsome men like you from time to time, but you don't have to worry because I won't be doing any kidnapping tonight."

He laughed also. Feeling a little more at ease with her, he relented. "Okay, now that I know I'm safe in your company, I'll take another glass of wine."

"That's more like it. Bartender, refill this handsome guy's glass."

The bartender obeyed. She asked him his name.

"Solomon," he said, "but before we go any further, you should know that I'm happily married."

She laughed again. "Relax, Solomon," she admonished with a smile. "I could tell you were married from your wedding ring. Trust me; I'm just trying to make small talk, nothing more."

"That's good to hear. It sorta shocked me when you started talking to me. It's not every day that a beautiful woman sits next to me in a bar, offers to buy me a drink, and starts a conversation."

"So you think I'm beautiful, do you?"

"Yes, I do!"

"Thanks! I think you're very handsome, but don't take that as a come-on."

"I won't. Anyway, if it were, it would be a waste of your time. Like I said, I'm happily married."

"Understood!"

"Good," he replied.

"What brings you to Washington?"

"I come here for a week each month to do consultant work for my company," he answered as he finished off the third glass of wine.

"What kind work do you do?"

"I'm in the information technology field."

"Sounds interesting, but it doesn't tell me much. Give me some details. What does your work entail?"

He began to answer her, but before he could explain any further about his work, he began to feel lightheaded and a little dizzy. He wasn't a serious alcohol drinker, and that third glass had pushed him past his limit.

She waited for him to respond. "Am I getting too much into your business?"

"No you're not," he answered.

Even though he wanted to continue talking with her with the hopes of finding out where they might have met in the past, the feeling of wooziness overtook him, leaving him with no other option except to call it a night. Besides, having her invade his space hadn't been in his plans. Her presence had totally changed the dynamics of the evening for him.

"I apologize, Evelyn," he said abruptly. "I totally get your interest in socializing; however, I'm really starting to feel a little tipsy from the extra glass of wine I drank. If you don't mind, I'm going to retire for the night."

"Are you sure it's the wine, or are you uncomfortable having an innocent conversation with a female bar mate because you're married?"

"Honestly, it's a little of both; however, it's mostly the wine," he said as he waved for the bartender to bring his bill.

"I told you already, I'm not trying to pick you up. You just seemed like someone who's nice to talk with."

"I hear you," he said, "but I still think it's best for me to call it a night. Have a great evening."

He paid his bill, got up from the stool, and walked out. Once he arrived back at his room, he plopped down on the bed trying to sober up. Lying there, he pondered back over the evening. Being around a woman had never caused him such uneasiness, yet tonight, for the first time, he'd felt anxious around another woman.

He realized how disappointed she'd been that he'd left. He'd seen it in her eyes as he walked out. Still, he felt he'd done the right thing by leaving. He definitely knew her from somewhere. However, since he couldn't figure out where, he felt it was best to forget about her, since he doubted that he'd ever run into her again.

———

The man who had been sitting next to Solomon had looked over at Evelyn with a smile, hoping that since Solomon was gone, she'd direct her attention toward him. However, Solomon's departure had turned her off from any desire to interact with someone else. Thus, she picked up her purse, paid the bartender, and left.

Back at her place, she settled onto the couch in front of her fireplace, struggling with her emotions. She was at a loss for words to explain why she felt so disappointed with Solomon's leaving and why she'd experienced an emotional void after his exit. She felt somewhat rejected by his leaving, although she couldn't understand why she felt that way. Her intent in going to the bar had been to socialize, not to become enchanted by a man, let alone a married one.

He probably did the right thing for both of us by leaving, she told herself. *Even with my best intentions, I'm better off not spending too much time talking to a married man.*

Still, she couldn't deny that his presence had an unexplainable pull on her. Neither was she able to shake the displeasure she felt at his walking out.

CHAPTER 5

The following month, on the second day of his trip to DC, as he was about to have dinner at his hotel, Evelyn walked out from one of the hotel conference rooms into the lobby. Seeing her again surprised him. He'd hoped that their paths wouldn't cross again, and now here she was in his environs once more.

Although she saw him too, she acted as if she didn't notice him.

She's probably ignoring me because she's still bothered by me leaving her at the bar, he reasoned.

Her feigning not to see him sharpened the guilt he was starting to feel. Wanting to make amends for the way her left her the last time, he grabbed her arm as she was about to walk past him.

"Hi," he said, hoping she'd at least let him offer her another apology.

"Well, if it's not the man who's afraid to have a friendly conversation with a woman because he's married. Don't worry; I'm not interested in buying you a drink or talking to you this time."

"Look, I'm extremely sorry for walking out on our conversation, but as I told you, I was starting to feel a bit intoxicated. Please accept my apologies."

"No problem," she responded in a grumpy tone, pulling her arm away from him and walking into the restroom.

It wasn't the best expression of forgiveness, but he accepted it. Believing again that he was better off staying away from her, he walked on into the restaurant. A few minutes later, she walked into the restaurant and sat alone at another table.

Wow, another shocker for the night. Not only has she found my hotel, but she's also decided to encroach upon my eating space.

Seeing her sitting there continued to make him feel lousy about the negative vibes he sensed between them. He wrestled with the thought of whether he should go over to her table and ask to join her for dinner. Then he noticed it, and it shook him. He continued his long, intense stare at her, not believing what he was seeing. He'd sensed there was something familiar about her, and now it was unveiled before his eyes.

She looks just like my mother!

He reached for his wallet and pulled out his mother's picture to be sure. His uncle had given him that picture after his mother's death, and he always kept it with him.

"Yep, it's true," he muttered.

The resemblance was bizarre. The coincidences were starting to unnerve him.

First, she entered the sports bar and sat next to me, disrupting my evening. Then she showed up in my hotel lobby, and afterward, in the restaurant where I'm dining, now, this uncanny resemblance to my mother. That's too many happenstances.

―――――

She noticed him staring at her, and it made her uncomfortable.

This guy is something else. First, he's afraid to talk to me. Now he's staring at me as if he's obsessed about something.

"Is there something wrong with me sitting here, since you keep staring at me?" she asked, somewhat angry.

He arose from his seat and walked over to her table.

"Are you eating alone?" he asked.

"Does that matter to you?" she replied sternly.

The circumstances were now reversed as he was trying to be sociable, and she was starting to feel uneasy.

"I was just wondering whether I could join you if you're eating alone."

"Are you sure a happily married man like you can handle sharing my company?" she asked.

Although for reasons she still couldn't explain, she was open to the prospect of getting to know him better, she wasn't interested if he wasn't going to be comfortable talking with her.

"Come on, give me a break. I've already apologized. Can't you see I'm trying to start over with you in a positive way?"

His sincerity and her unexplained attraction to him easily softened her.

"Okay, it would be nice having some company."

He sat down, and she quickly started a conversation. Dinner offered her the opportunity to provide him with a microscopic view of her life. She was twenty-eight years old and had grown up in Richmond with her mother and three older brothers. Since she had a natural gift for engaging people, to take advantage of her people skills, she attended Howard University, majoring in public relations.

In her second year at Howard, she met her husband-to-be, Jim Clark, at a restaurant in Georgetown. He was eighteen years older, and she liked that fact. He was the father she missed and the lover she needed. Jim was an MIT graduate with a master's degree in urban planning and a concentration in international development. He provided consultant services to the army. Mainly, he helped rebuild war zones after the bombing ended and the peace started. By her own admission, she was the aggressor.

"Although Jim was white, he was so handsome, I couldn't resist at least saying hello," she admitted.

Her conversations with Jim led to more dates and marriage six months later. Four years following marriage, a roadside bomb exploded in Afghanistan, killing him and three other soldiers.

"I crawled into a deep emotional hole afterward," she said. "His life-insurance policy and other benefits were more than enough to keep me going financially, while antidepressant drugs kept me during the many months I holed up inside my town house. My psychiatrist recommended that I end my prolonged mourning period and get on with the business of living. The day I met you in the bar was my first step back into the social scene I once loved. Putting the past behind me was hard, but I was excited about starting life over again. After you rejected my attempts to be sociable and walked out, I went back home, feeling the need to crawl back into my depression, but I resisted. I couldn't let one person take me back down that gloomy road again."

"I understand losing someone you care about. I lost my mother when I was six," he revealed with a touch of sadness.

Feeling empathy for the pain he'd unclothed with his admission, she reached over and gently rubbed the top of his hand. "I'm sorry," she said.

"It's okay. Mostly, I've moved past it emotionally. Except some days I start missing her again."

"I know what you mean," she said. "I guess we have something in common; we both have tragically lost a loved one."

"I guess we do," he replied. "Interestingly, you have an uncanny resemblance to my mother."

He took out the picture of his mother and showed it to her. She looked at the picture and then gave him a puzzled look.

"Wow, this is unbelievable," she said.

"It really is, isn't it?"

She laughed. "Life is unpredictable. We meet at a bar, run into each other at this hotel, and then you discover that I look like your mother. Isn't that a weird set of coincidences?"

"That's the same thing I've been saying to myself," he said with a chuckle.

"Maybe that's a positive sign. Maybe we're kindred spirits that were meant to meet. Maybe our meeting is destiny." *Maybe that's why I'm drawn to you*, she thought but didn't dare say.

He shrugged his shoulders. "Maybe!"

She continued to share her life story with him. Once they finished eating, she thanked him for joining her for dinner.

"No problem. I'll cover the bill," he said as she was reaching for it.

"Thanks," she uttered as she leaned over and kissed him on his cheek.

Driving back home, she thought about their time together. *That picture of his mother was too deep*, she thought.

Although she definitely felt something mystifying about the two encounters she'd had with him, dining with him had increased his appeal to her—a feeling she hoped would soon dissipate. She knew that getting caught up with a married man rarely led to a happy ending. Therefore, she decided to stay away from his hotel to avoid running into him again. Yet a part of her secretly hoped their paths would cross once more.

———

Solomon went back to his room to talk with Jan without mentioning anything about his evening or Evelyn. After finishing their talk, he lay back on the bed as thoughts of the evening passed in and out of his mind. He thought of the concept of serendipity and the way good fortunes often occurred by coincidence. Yet something in him felt that meeting her might not foretell good fortune but rather trouble.

Destiny!

He thought of her explanation for their meeting again. It was the first of many times she'd use that word to explain their strange encounters.

Maybe she was right. Maybe there's something more to meeting her than chance.

He hoped it wasn't destiny. He hoped he wouldn't keep running into her. His world was without drama, and he wanted it to stay that way. Still, he couldn't overcome the wonderment of her likeness to his mother. That fact still gripped him.

CHAPTER 6

Two months following their dinner at his hotel, he ran into Evelyn again, this time as he was leaving the building where he worked. He couldn't believe his eyes as he saw her walking in his direction.

This is too much of a coincidence!

Running into her again was starting to make him suspicious that these were more than mere occurrences. Then he observed that she seemed as surprised to see him as he was to see her, even as her face lit with a smile upon noticing him.

"Let's get this straight; I'm not stalking you," she said, walking up to him and laughing. "Although I did hope to see you once more, and here you are. Like I said before, maybe it's our destiny to get to know each other."

There was that word again.

Destiny!

The idea was starting to bother him.

"You work around here?" he asked, trying to understand how she just happened to end up in that part of the city at that particular time.

"No, I don't. Here's an even bigger shocker: I'm rarely in this part of town. Yet for some reason, I had the urge to visit a thrift shop nearby. I swear, I had no idea I'd run into you, but I'm glad I did. Maybe that's why something steered me in this direction today—just so I could see you again. Having dinner with you the last time was great. I enjoyed being out, and I especially enjoyed your company."

He couldn't believe that she was feeling elated about seeing him again, but he couldn't deny it, and it made him feel uncomfortable. He wondered again if running into her again was truly accidental or if it was intentional.

Destiny!

He wasn't sure about that.

Doesn't she remember I'm married? What's her real agenda?

A host of questions went through his mind.

"What, you're not excited to see me, too?" she inquired.

"I'm certainly surprised," he answered, still trying to comprehend what was happening in his world and why this woman kept showing up in it.

"That's not what I asked you. Are you excited to see me, too?" she asked again pushing him for an answer.

In truth, he did feel some delight sprinkled in with the anxieties that stumbling into her caused.

"Yes, I'm happy to see you again," he answered reluctantly.

"I knew you were," she said exuberantly as she wrapped her arms around him and pressed herself hard against his chest.

He gently pushed her back from him.

"Where are you on way to? he asked.

"Before running into you, I had no particular plans except, like I said before, doing some shopping. Are you hungry? I am. Let's have dinner together again. I know a great restaurant near here."

A part of him knew that her suggestion was outside his comfort zone, but he kept telling himself that he didn't need to be overprotective. Underestimating the growing electricity between them was a mistake he'd later regret.

Seeing his hesitation, she pressed her hand into his and pulled him along as she walked in the direction of the restaurant.

"Don't worry, my married friend; you're safe with me," she said, and off they went. It was their first intentional outing together, but it wouldn't be their last.

At dinner, he continued to talk about how much she resembled his mother.

"It's weird, I must admit, but you can be assured that I'm not the reincarnation of your mother," she said with a giggle.

He laughed. "I didn't think you were my mother returned; it's just that the resemblance is surreal. In fact, everything in my short time of knowing you has been surreal. These chance encounters have me puzzled."

"Me too. Accept it; we were destined to know each other, so let's flow with it."

"That's easy for you to say. You're single, but I'm married, remember? I can't just flow anywhere. I have to know where the flow is taking me and make sure I'm not creating problems for myself."

"You're right; you are married. I've never been in the business of hanging out with a married man, but here I am doing just that and, strangely, wanting more of it. Regardless of what happens in our flow going forward, I want you to be assured that I understand the risk that our being together poses to your marriage."

Her response gave him some emotional ease, but nothing she could say eliminated the uneasiness he experienced from being around her.

After dinner, she handed him a piece of paper with her phone number on it. "Give me a call, and let's find other exciting things to do when you're in town."

"I'll think about it," he said.

"That's good enough for me," she replied.

CHAPTER 7

The next month, when she thought he'd probably be in town, she made an evening call to his hotel and asked to be connected to his room.

"Hello."

"Hi, Solomon."

"Evelyn?"

"Yes. How are you?"

"I'm great. What are you doing calling my room?"

"I just wanted to check on you. I thought that you might want to get out from that hotel this week and go somewhere for fun. What are you doing tomorrow night? I got two tickets to a Bob James concert at Blues Alley, and my girlfriend informed me at the last minute that she can't go with me."

"Look, where are you trying to go with this? If we keep hanging out together, it's going to create problems for both of us."

She understood the same. Yet she couldn't explain what was happening to her. She didn't plan for this growing gravitation toward him. It wasn't as if she hadn't been trying to resist his pull. However, the seeds of captivation, there from the first moment she met him at the bar, had only intensified.

"Look, I know a growing friendship between us has the potential of becoming complicated. However, what I'm feeling is different from anything I've ever experienced before. Maybe I'm totally wrong, but I feel compelled to continue building the connection we're establishing. I don't know why we were supposed to meet, but I want to keep getting to know you more as we find out. I'm not looking for intimacy; I just want to stay on the path of discovering why we were brought into each other's life. I got an extra ticket; that's a fact. But if you're not interested in going, I understand."

He thought about it.

"This scares me. I shouldn't be entertaining this idea. At some point, I'll have to pay a price if I continue to let our relationship develop any further. Plus if my wife, Jan, found out about us spending time together, she'd be furious."

"But you are giving it some thought, and that should tell you that something real is going on here. Under any other circumstances, would you be wrestling with yourself about whether or not you should go out with another woman?"

"Absolutely not; going anywhere with a woman other than my wife would've never crossed my mind."

"I believe you, Solomon. I know you're not the type of man who would fool around."

"Then why tempt me with this offer?"

"I don't know. This is not the normal me either. I've never been attracted to a married man, but I'm drawn to you in a way I'm not able to explain or resist. Look, I want you to come with me. I know you would enjoy the concert, but if you don't want to go, as I said before, I'll understand. You don't have to feel any pressure. Just do what makes sense for you."

"I'll be honest with you; I'm captivated by you also," he said. "That's what frightens me about you, Evelyn. We both know this is moving us in a direction that we may regret later."

He was right, but she'd always been open to taking risks, albeit not this type of risk. Yet, something inside her felt that getting to know him better was a risk worth taking.

He thought about it some more.

"I know I should take a pass on this invitation, but for some reason, the word *no* can't come out of my mouth."

Finally, after losing the battle with his conscience, he said, "Why not. Bob James is one of my favorite jazz musicians."

"Great," she said happily. "I'll come by and pick you up."

"No," he said, "I'll just meet you there."

"Are you sure? It's no problem for me to come and get you."

"Thanks, but I can meet you there."

"Okay, Solomon. I'll see you out front of the club at eight."

———

The concert was more enjoyable than he'd anticipated. Bob James and his jazz combo were at their best musically, and Evelyn was wild and energetic, screaming and yelling throughout the performance like a cheerleader. She was different from Jan, who was more subdued, although Jan certainly knew how to enjoy herself.

The band reveled in the audience's appreciation of their music. Bob James specifically thanked the woman in the blue pantsuit. To which Evelyn yelled back, "Thank you too, Bob!" Solomon could only look at her and smile. She was definitely different but exciting.

Jan called a couple of times during the concert. He knew she'd be concerned that he hadn't called her since leaving work. He'd told her earlier when they talked that he was getting something to eat after work and would call her immediately afterward, and he always kept his promises to her. Feeling anxious, he picked up the phone as soon as he got back to his room, knowing he couldn't tell her the truth about the night.

"What the hell happened to you?" she asked, obviously concerned. "You didn't call me back like you promised, and that's not like you."

"Sorry, one of the guys from the company came by the hotel as I was eating and said he wanted to add a little spice to my visit, so he gave me a ticket to the Bob James concert at Blues Alley. I rushed out to catch the concert, and the place was so loud, I decided to wait until I got back to my room before I called you."

"Bob James, huh? I'm still a little perturbed that you hadn't called me, but I'm glad you did something fun while you were there. All that going to work and going back to the hotel is boring," she said, letting go of her anger and concern. "Thanks for calling. I'm glad to know you had a good time. Get some rest, and let's talk in the morning. A few more days, and I'll be back in your arms again."

"I look forward to that," he replied.

Once the phone call ended, he climbed into his bed, exhausted from a long day. A line from Warren L. G. De Mills's poem came to his mind:

There is something mystical about her, in the manner of seduction.

There was indeed something mysterious about Evelyn, and for the first time since being married, he felt an allure for another woman. Over the next three days, he thought about calling her, but he felt spending time with her at the concert was enough risk for one trip.

CHAPTER 8

During his next visit, as soon as he arrived at his hotel, he called her to say he was in town and just wanted to say hello.

"You don't have to justify calling me Solomon. I knew you would call. I expected it."

He wanted to ask her how she knew but decided against it. He was certain she'd say fate, destiny, or something along those lines. He was even starting to believe her himself. She was now occupying a space inside him; that much was certain. The fact that he'd called her revealed the power of his attraction to her.

Although he'd made the call, he had no expectations, nor any idea where the call would lead, nor if he wanted it to lead anywhere. There was only the inner urge, the compulsion to call her. What was the force behind his irresistible attraction to her? He didn't know. However, he wasn't surprised that she wasn't surprised he'd called.

"You like literature, right?" she asked.

"I love it. How did you know that?"

"Your soul told me."

That's scary! he thought. *Everything about this woman is scary and risky.*

"Well, your intuition is correct. Why do you ask?"

"There's a poetry event I want to take you to. I know you'd like it. It's this evening. Can you make it?"

As usual, he hesitated. Understanding his delay, she waited for him to process the decisions he continued to confront in dealing with her. He was glad she understood his inner struggles and was willing to be patient as he reconciled his conflicts. One inner voice stated all the familiar concerns and uneasiness that he should've heeded, but a stronger voice encouraged him to continue with their flow.

"What time should I be ready?"

"If you're going to be working at the same building where I ran into you before, then I'll be there with a taxi to pick you up as soon as you get off. That's five p.m., right?"

"Yes," he said.

"Okay, I'll see you then."

———

Promptly at 5:00 p.m., he walked out of the building, entered into the waiting taxi, and they headed off, first to dinner and then to the Pyramid Atlantic Art Center on Georgia Avenue. He called Jan from the taxi to say he was going to dinner and would call her later.

Evelyn smiled as he made the call. "Your wife is a special woman, isn't she?"

"She's very special, and one of a kind."

"I can tell there's tenderness between you and Jan. You love her greatly, don't you?"

"Yes, I do. That's the reason I don't know why I'm doing this. If I lost her, it would be the end of my world."

She rested her head on his shoulders and wrapped her arms around his.

"I understand," she said, again not knowing what else to say.

"I'm happy to see the love you feel for your wife. She's blessed to have a man like you, strong and yet gentle and caring."

Again, he was comforted by knowing that she understood what his marriage meant to him.

Dinner was at Mulebone, an upscale restaurant with a southern flavor. Solomon liked the place, and he especially liked the food. He was glad they went there first as he wanted the opportunity for them to talk. They sat down and ordered drinks and then food. The waiter brought the wine first. As they waited for dinner, he sat back and clasped his hands together.

"What are we doing, Evelyn?"

"I can only tell you what I'm doing."

"Fair enough; then what are you doing?"

She leaned forward in her chair. "Something I never thought I'd be doing; falling for a married man."

He was about to respond, but she pressed her fingers against his lips, gesturing for him to keep silent and let her finish expressing herself.

"I'm aware of all the taboos regarding our budding relationship, and I'm certainly aware of the risks it poses to your marriage as well as the risks it poses to my fragile heart. I wish I could walk away from you, from us, and these feelings for you that only keep getting stronger, but in all truthfulness, I can't. Neither can I explain why I can't."

He could see the sincerity in her eyes as she spoke.

"I'm in a place that I've never been in before, experiencing feelings I could never imagine experiencing for a married man, and I don't know what to do about it. Therefore, what I'm doing is flowing with it, hoping that things will get clearer for me further along this journey with you. I do know this much: I've never felt for any man what's been swelling up inside me for you. It's different, and it's special. All I can hope is that you will let us continue our flow together, even though I know it's even harder and more challenging for you because of your marriage. I know you don't want to do anything that will cause you to lose a woman who's special to you. I don't want you to lose her either; neither do I want us to stop spending time together."

She leaned back in her chair. "What are you doing, Solomon?"

"I don't know. I'm not sure of what I'm doing. I don't even recognize myself anymore. I've been swept up in the grip of feelings I too don't totally understand. The man I thought I was wouldn't be here with you, yet here I am."

He paused for a moment, closed his eyes, and inhaled deeply.

"Maybe I'm reading too much into this. Up to this point, we haven't kissed, or made love. It's only been a close friendship. However, I'm not used to this type of friendship with a woman. Couple with that, I haven't been able to tell Jan about you and our time together at all, which is another sign of what's dangerous about our bond: the secrecy."

"I hear you. Let's just keep our flow going and see where we end up. As you said, so far, it's only been a close friendship, nothing more. If it makes you feel better, tell Jan about it. At this point you haven't done anything wrong, other than a few outings."

"I wished it was that easy, but we both know it's not. There is no way I can tell Jan about us now. We just have to be careful and not allow our relationship to go any further than where it is."

He knew that accomplishing that feat would be hard, but he needed to convince himself that it was possible.

Once they finished eating, they headed to the Pyramid. When they arrived and he saw the billboard, he couldn't believe his eyes. The poetry performance was being given by Warren De Mills with an attending jazz band. He looked at her with a smile of delight.

Her face said back to him, "Yes, I know you like his poetry."

He wrapped his arms around her waist, and they went inside and settled into their seats. Before long, Warren was chanting a soothing poetic utterance that flowed in harmony with the rhythms of his band.

You infatuate my soul like the playground to a child...

He was enthralled by the words floating on sounds and the thought of the two of them experiencing this special moment together. He settled back into his seat, relaxed, and savored the moment. He was flowing with her as she'd asked him to, and as he settled into their flow, the melodious harmony of the moment lured him into surrender.

Warren continued: *Maybe her spirit has possessed my heart...*

Resisting their flow was now no longer an option.

Yes, his soul said as Warren and the music carried their flow along. *Yes!*

He looked over at her, and she looked back at him, happy for what she saw in his eyes. He was gaining peace about traveling this journey with her.

CHAPTER 9

The idea of his marriage and the inner contradictions that being with Evelyn created for him couldn't deter Solomon's desire to be with her. She'd aroused in him something that he'd never imagined he could feel for a woman other than his wife. In both their minds, something so deep and tender couldn't be wrong. It had been a year since they first met and started spending time together, and their allure for each other was now intense. While he hadn't committed the final act of marital infidelity, it was just a matter of time. He craved her, and she him.

It was early March, and they'd spent the evening in revelry at the Mardi Gras celebration on K Street. They were a bit intoxicated and she suggested they go back to her place and sober up with coffee. Tipsy and still frolicking, they stumbled into her town house and fell onto her living-room couch. It was an awkward moment as she landed on top of him.

Briefly, they looked into each other's eyes; then, before he could move to get up, her tongue penetrated deeply into his mouth. He resisted at first, trying to resolve the guilt in his soul with the fire raging inside.

No!

Yes!

The war raged within him. However, the passion of her kisses pulled him deep into the place of no return. Then, finally, shutting out all concerns about his marriage, he yielded to a moment whose time had come.

Feeling his surrender, she kissed him even more passionately. Her soft lips and moist tongue traveled slowly from his mouth to his cheeks, neck, and back again. He knew she hungered for his embrace. She'd wanted this moment, longed for it, and waited patiently for it to happen. Therefore, immersed in this consecration of their love, he knew she yielded to it with no regrets, finally releasing the affections she had been struggling to contain.

Aroused, he began to touch her, causing her to tremble as his fingers moved down her back to her thighs and legs. The Mardi Gras dress she wore had a split in it, and underneath she was wearing a satin G-string panty. He placed his hand inside the split and traced the lines of the G-string. She moaned.

"It's been a long time since I've felt a man's touch."

He continued slowly, gaining confidence as he went. He pulled her G-string to the side. Feeling her moisture, he placed a finger inside her. She sighed heavily from the titillating fire of arousal his touch inflamed.

Sensing that she was about to be pulled over the edge, she grabbed his hand from underneath her panty, unbuttoned his shirt, and started kissing his chest. As she continued kissing down his chest, she unbuckled his belt and pulled off his pants and boxers. His firmness was apparent.

Again, he attempted to pull her off him; however, resisting his efforts, she climbed atop him, lifted his stiffness, and gently slid herself down on it. Aroused at the fill of him, she cried out, "My Solomon." Then she stroked up and down slowly upon the hardness inside her until she reached the pinnacle. He soon followed.

Still atop him, she leaned down and kissed him affectionately some more. Then, with her desires gratified, she climbed off him and lay on his chest. He wrapped his arms around her and held her tightly. Their initiation into the world of forbidden love was now complete.

"I love you," she murmured.

"Likewise," he responded.

After a few minutes, she drifted off into sleep. He, in contrast, couldn't rest. Despite the gratifications of the moment, he knew they were now treading in troubling waters. He slid from under her, walked to the window, and stared into the darkness outside. He then turned and looked back at her as she rested peacefully.

He realized how much his life had changed since meeting Evelyn. Before then, he could have been the featured story in a success magazine—a black man making it against the odds. Growing up in the Austin neighborhood on the Far West Side of Chicago, he was an only child who had never known his father. Then, tragically, his mother had died in a car accident when he was six, a traumatic event that left deep emotional yearnings. Bereft of parents, he spent his early childhood shuffled among different relatives—first to some aunts and then finally an uncle (to whom he grew very close), who stepped in and became the surrogate father and male guide he needed.

Austin started out as a community of immigrant families and then underwent a dramatic demographic shift brought on by white flight. By his teenage years, Austin had become an economic ghost town. With few opportunities for young black men like him, youth gangs and violence became the visible signs of adolescent hopelessness and despair amid community decay.

Yet, despite growing up among the dangers that befell many of his peers, he not only survived but also constructed a pathway out from misfortune into a life of success. Through the strict rearing and the mentoring of his uncle, he'd matured into a man with a healthy mental outlook and corresponding values, along with a deep set of principles that served as his code of ethical conduct. As a result, he earned a scholarship to college and graduated cum laude, found the vocation that represented a fulfilling life's calling, and wedded a woman who cherished him. From time to time, minor turbulence had caused a few bumps; however, mostly, the ride of his life had been smooth.

Until a year ago, he'd been faithful to what his uncle referred to as the rules of engagement for a dangerous environment. Then it all changed. At the start of his relationship with Evelyn, he neither had known his vulnerabilities nor realized his emotional susceptibilities or the limits of his willpower when confronted with her allure. Neither had he comprehended the power of her attraction. However, watching her laying naked, it was all in full view to him now.

He'd tried to resist the pull he felt from her. He'd thought he could keep their interactions confined within the barriers of friendship without benefits, but he'd been merely lying to himself. The force and power of his attraction to her was greater than his resistance. He thought of the line by Llàrjme.

If she had looked into his eyes at that very moment, she would have seen the inferno that she had thrown him into.

Standing there observing her, he could feel the weight of stress upon him. He was caught up in an entanglement he didn't know how to resolve. All those years prior to meeting her, he'd been prudent and cautious, taking great care to avoid dangers by making good decisions. Now, here he was taking risks and moving from a secure place to the edges. Now, the strings that had bound the guarded world he'd lived in were loosening, and for the first time, he was terrified, taking steps on a path he didn't know and flowing in directions of which he wasn't certain. Although it was clear they'd traveled too far, their flow now seemed irreversible, and he had no clue as to what he should do next.

He sensed he was heading into the eye of a storm, and with that sense, he could feel a gripping inner turmoil. Yet he couldn't see any way of avoiding the storm that lay ahead. Climbing up from the world of betrayal he'd descended into would be difficult. Nevertheless, he knew that continuing down this path with her would only be seismic, which would rip his marriage apart. Imagining life without his wife tormented him. He understood

Evelyn couldn't remain a part of his world, and although a part of him couldn't let her go, he knew that eventually he'd have to find his way back to his true self and say good-bye to her.

Today, however, wasn't that day. Therefore, he walked back over to her, climbed back onto the couch, and pulled her back into his arms, deciding to let go of his troubles and be contented for one night in the love of two women.

PART THREE

Back in the present

CHAPTER 10

Solomon woke as the plane shook from turbulence. He knew that when his flight landed, Evelyn would be at the airport waiting. That too was a part of his monthly ritual. He understood that for her their growing closeness wasn't problematic. She loved filling the space his being away from Chicago and Jan provided them. Even though she knew he loved Jan and would never leave her, she was happy sharing life with him.

For him, it was just the opposite. In the words of Molly Ringle, *Being around her now was nine parts bliss and one part torment.* No matter how much time he spent with her or how close they became, he couldn't overcome his constant guilt. Although she never pressured him regarding his marriage or asked him to give her more than what they possessed—their five days of love per month—the guilt for him was persistent and nagging.

In another world, one without Jan in it, she would have been just as perfect a wife for him as Jan was now. Unfortunately, in the world he lived in, there was no way they could remain lovers. To hold on to her would mean continuing to risk losing everything that was important to him. Therefore, as much as she meant to him, this morning on the balcony he'd made up his mind that this trip to DC would be his last. He would ask the company to send a representative to replace him, and he would painfully tell Evelyn that their affair was over. Then he could put this mistake behind him, spend more time with Jan, and restore himself back to the old, faithful Solomon.

He put on his headset and turned up his iPod as he prepared himself for the painful moments ahead. Ironically, Evelyn's favorite song by Sade was playing.

You're ruling the way that I move, and I breathe your air.

The plane started its descent!

CHAPTER 11

Evelyn threw her purse strap over her shoulder and headed out the door to her car. She didn't know what to expect from this day, especially with matters of the heart involved. She'd just have to wait and find out later how it would all turn out. She'd invested much of herself into her love affair with Solomon, and although the possibility of a divestiture was real, she desperately wanted to avoid it, knowing how emotionally devastating losing him would be for her.

Regrets knocked at the door of her heart, yet she refused to answer. She'd felt no regrets in the past and wouldn't allow herself to have any now. She understood the reasons for the choices she'd made, and given the same circumstances, she'd make those same choices again and again.

If there would be any regrets, it would be for the painful guilt that plagued Solomon about their relationship. Lately, his inner struggles had become more obvious, although he'd been more reserved and less willing to discuss his feelings with her. Thus, she wondered what was going on in his mind. Beyond expressing the constant guilt he felt from their relationship, he hadn't shared anything more about what he was feeling inside.

I hope that on this trip, I can get him to open up and let me inside. Maybe then, I can convince him to see things my way. It would be better for him, for us, if he could see things my way, she thought.

It was a challenging time for the two of them, but she was determined to remain strong.

Holding on to the love of a man is real work, the voice inside her head uttered. *Yes, it is, but he's worth the work,* she affirmed from a place deep within her heart. *He's truly worth the work.*

Again, she concluded she had no regrets. She was happy with the patterns into which her life had been woven. The only thing important to her now was holding on to the most valuable treasure life had ever given to her. Throughout their three years together, she'd believed their relationship could last, even under the unique circumstances it existed, but now she wasn't so sure. Still, she held firm to the belief that meeting him was no accident, no mistake.

Things happen in ways we can never imagine for reasons we can't always understand.

That was her mantra, and she held unwaveringly to it. For her, everything in life happened by design and purpose, although those designs and purposes often remained hidden from her understanding. She was especially sure that their love was intended. Therefore, she was determined to hold on to that love until whatever was meant for them fully unfolded.

She returned to thinking about the risks their relationship faced. Then she realized how much time had passed while she wallowed in thoughts about something beyond her control in the moment. It was a busy day, and she needed to get going.

She shook the concerns about their future from her mind, knowing that all she could do was wait and see how things would turn out.

As she drove along, making her way through the city, she mused again about the way things unfolded in life.

Who could have predicted that my odyssey would have taken me along the paths it did?

Before long, she arrived at the airport. Waiting for Solomon to exit, she engaged in a final moment of reflection.

Matters of the heart can be complicated, her inner woman muttered. *Matters of the heart! Only time will tell.*

CHAPTER 12

Jan had been asleep for a while before the phone rang and awakened her. She saw it was Solomon. Knowing him, she guessed he was calling to let her know he'd arrived safely.

"Hi, so you made it," she said, pretending that everything was okay.

"Yes. It was the usual bumpy flight, but I'm here safely. It just landed and I wanted to call you before I got my bags and headed to my hotel. How was your ride to work?"

"Oh, I'm not at work yet. I'm still at home."

"Why? Are you all right? Is there something wrong?"

"Nothing's wrong. I'm okay. I was just feeling a little nauseous, but I'm fine now. In fact, I'll be walking out the door in a few minutes."

"A little nauseous, huh?" he said, jokingly. "Do you have a surprise for me?" he asked, laughing.

"Don't even go there," she said, laughing too. "You know there's no bread baking in this oven."

"Darn," he said, and they both laughed again.

"Solomon, I found a receipt for a dinner cruise in your jacket when I was straightening out your closet. What was that for?"

"Oh, that," he said. "One of the staff here had a birthday. I purchased that dinner cruise for him and his wife as a birthday gift."

Hearing that answer from him brought her the needed emotional relief while making her feel embarrassed about the suspicions she'd allowed to consume her thoughts. Whether his answer was true or not, it was what she wanted to hear.

"Is everything okay, Jan?"

"Yes, everything is fine. I'm glad you made it safely, and I'm certainly glad to hear your voice. I look forward to talking to you later this evening."

"Me too! Have a good day at work."

"Okay, I will."

With that, they both hung up, and Jan hurried out the door.

———

After the call to Jan, Solomon could feel his stomach tightening and his pulse racing.

Jan's discovery of that receipt could have been a costly mistake for me.

He was glad she accepted his explanation. However, he was starting to fret that she might become suspicious of him and that she might eventually find out about his involvement with Evelyn. He certainly didn't want that to happen, especially now that he'd made up his mind to end his affair. Her finding that receipt was a clear indication that he was right to break off his relationship with Evelyn before it cost him dearly.

CHAPTER 13

Seeing Solomon exiting the terminal and heading toward her car caused Evelyn's face to beam with joy. She lived for his visits. When he wasn't in town, she engrossed herself in her work as an events planner, a business he'd suggested she establish. However, when he came to town, he took priority over everything.

Once he entered the car, she leaned over to hug and kiss him.

"How was the flight?" she asked.

"It was okay. We need to talk today after work."

His words caused fear to swell up inside her. She understood that for his sake, they would eventually have to end their romance, yet she dreaded the thought of not having him.

"I'm helping the Ghanaian Embassy host a gala honoring a businessman from South Africa, and I need to be there tonight to help coordinate the affair. Do you mind if we talked afterward?" she asked worriedly.

"No problem. Just come by my hotel room when you finish."

"I would rather you join me tonight. Being there could garner you some valuable international business contacts. Remember, you always talked about wanting to do business in Africa."

"Okay, pick me up from my room then. What time does it start?"

"Seven. I hope you don't mind, but I bought you an African suit for the evening since everyone will be dressed in African garb."

"Its fine, Evelyn."

Soon they arrived at his hotel.

"Do you want me to come up with you?"

"No, I'm just going to check in, drop my bags, and head to the office. I'll see you this evening."

She kissed him again, and he exited the car. As she drove away, she sensed that her time of kissing him was ending. Riding to her office, she began projecting in her mind the conversation she expected they would have later.

Evelyn. Although knowing and loving you has been special, I can't go any further with this. I've tried—you know I have—to live in the moment and flow with the feelings I have for you, but I can't bear the guilt of our relationship, and the constant lying to Jan I've had to do since we began seeing each other. I'm sorry, but I just can't do it anymore. This is not for me; this isn't how I want to live.

I wish we could have met during another time and under another set of circumstances, but it just wasn't in the cards. I belong to someone whom I love a lot, and I don't want to lose her. Losing Jan would devastate me. I don't want to lose you either, but in the world we live in, I can't have you both without keeping to this path of dishonesty, and I can't do that anymore. It pains me deeply, but I've no choice; I have to walk away from our journey together. It's a heartbreaking choice, but it's my only choice.

You said it was our destiny to love each other. I just don't see that. What power would bring us together with no real chance of freely expressing the love we have for each other? Who would choose such a destiny for us? I certainly wouldn't. If we'd lived in a different world and I could choose our destiny, I'd want us to spend a lifetime together, not only as lovers but also as husband and wife instead of this one-week-per-month thing we have going on now. However, that option is not available to us, and it will never be available to us. Therefore, we just have to do the right thing and let each other go.

She imagined that after the initial pain of hearing him, she would respond.

I understand, Solomon. I've always understood the pain our relationship caused you. The man you've always seen yourself as prior to meeting me was never capable of creating the space for us to exist in love. Yet can you deny that there's another man inside you who's touched by us, moved by our love, and compelled by the pull of our hearts and soul?

You've always been conflicted about our relationship, and in many ways so have I. Nevertheless, I don't regret loving you, but

I do accept that it is time for the war within you to end. Does our surrender in this moment mean that we were not destined to love each other? I don't think so. Rather, for me, it means that our love just doesn't fit into a normal box. What box it fits in I'm not sure, but I still feel that there's a space for you and me, and that's why we met and discovered an irresistible love for each other. My desire is that we continue to explore where that space exists, but for your sake, I'll walk away if that's what you really want me to do.

When the voices in her head quieted, a few teardrops appeared in her eyes, small cracks in her emotional dam. Moments later the drops became trickles, and eventually a river of tears began to stream down her face. She pulled the car over to the side and parked. Consumed in this moment of lamentation, she cried out to her soul.

Why bring us together and not provide our love with the opportunity to flourish and grow? What's the point of us meeting and loving only to lose each other?

Crying and beating on the steering wheel, she felt all the confidence she had in their love washing away in a flow of anguish.

Then, mysteriously, calm came, and from the calm clarity as her soul spoke back to her.

The flow of a river traverses across rocks, leaps down rapids, and even becomes waterfalls as it meanders toward its destination. She who is carried by the river must trust its flow until it reaches the end.

From that inner voice, her faith returned. The message was clear. Although this moment would be trying for them and their love, even if they had to part for a period, she must never stop trusting that a greater purpose had led them to each other and that somehow their love would endure and find its proper space. With a new sense of peace, she wiped her eyes, composed herself, and started again toward her office.

"I love you, Solomon, and I'll never let you leave my heart, no matter what," she declared aloud.

CHAPTER 14

At six o'clock, Evelyn arrived at Solomon's hotel. She'd had his clothes delivered earlier. She knew he'd be ready, because promptness was one of his strong character traits. As he emerged from the hotel lobby looking like royalty in his African attire, she beamed with approval.

"You look good, my African prince."

"Thank you, my African princess!"

"Solomon, no matter what happens later when we talk, let's make tonight a special night together."

"Okay, my love," he said compliantly.

Once they arrived at the event, she went to talk with the embassy staff to check on how the plans for the evening were going. He looked around, impressed by what he saw. Obviously, Evelyn and the embassy team had put much work into organizing this event. There was lots of food, plenty to drink, and great entertainment. Judging by the number of dignitaries in attendance—African ambassadors, a representative from the mayor's office, a few African American congressmen, business executives, and leaders of several national black organizations—it certainly seemed like a who's who event for African and African American VIPs.

The honored guest must be an important man, he thought.

He grabbed a glass of wine and found a place in the corner to withdraw from the others. He wasn't as good at socializing as Evelyn, and besides, he wasn't in the mood for much mingling since he couldn't stop thinking about the conversation he needed to have with Evelyn later. He dreaded it, but it was necessary. It was time to end something that never should've started.

Yet, despite his attempt to avoid interacting with others, throughout the evening, people came over to him to make introductions or attempt small talk. However, preoccupied with pressing matters of the heart, he remained distant. After about thirty minutes of being aloof, a woman came up and introduced herself.

"Hi, my name is Nandi. I'm the wife of Jonas, the businessperson who's being honored tonight. I expect him to be here soon."

"Good to meet you. My name is Solomon, and I'm here as a guest of Evelyn, one of the people who helped to organize this affair."

"Oh yes, I've met Evelyn. She's a special soul," Nandi responded.

"Yes, she is," he said.

Nandi made a few more attempts to chat with him and, afterward, left him sitting there. Before long, Jonas Nkosi and his entourage arrived. Solomon looked for Nandi, but apparently, she'd disappeared.

The entourage consisted of eight people, including a woman who held on to Jonas's arm in a way that appeared strange to Solomon.

Who could that be? he wondered.

He thought the woman might be Jonas's personal assistant, but even if she was, she clung close to Jonas in a way that suggested to Solomon that the two were in an intimate relationship. He worked with executives, so he was no stranger to the illicit relationships many executives formed with their close assistants. After a few minutes of analyzing the two, he decided to leave the judgment of Jonas's relationship with the woman on his arms to others. Yet he couldn't help but notice that even as they began to mingle with the many dignitaries, the woman stayed on his arm, unashamedly.

Whoever she is to him, they're not trying to hide their closeness from anyone in the room, including his wife.

After making their rounds of introduction with Evelyn as their host, Jonas and the woman finally made it over to where Solomon was disengaging himself from everyone else.

"Mr. Nkosi, this is Solomon, my dearest friend. Solomon, this is Jonas Nkosi, our honored guest, and this is his wife, Tabisa."

Wife!

The words jolted Solomon.

"Wife," he blared aloud. Then he laughed.

Evelyn frowned, puzzled by his behavior. Jonas crinkled his forehead, confused about what Solomon found so amusing.

"If this is your wife, you should know that there's someone else here also pretending to be your wife," he said.

At that time, Nandi walked up and grabbed Jonas's hand.

"This is the person I was speaking of," he said, pointing to Nandi, stunned that she had the audacity to actually reappear, with Jonas and his real wife standing there.

Jonas, Nandi, and Tabisa smiled at Solomon.

"Nandi is also my wife. They both are," Jonas said, pointing to the two women. "In my country, having more than one wife is a part of our culture and tradition, although there're still some people who frown upon it."

Although Jonas continued talking, Solomon was not listening. The words *they both are* had caused his to mind zone out.

They both are!

The words rang in his head like the after-effect of an explosion. As a result, he totally lost his grip on the moment. He was no longer cognizant that he was holding something in his hand; the glass of wine he held fell and shattered, drawing the attention of others in the room.

"Are you all right?" Jonas asked.

"Solomon, what's the matter?" Evelyn inquired with a sense of worry.

However, he remained muted, buried in a daze. When he returned to consciousness, he saw the many eyes looking on at him in concern. Now embarrassed, he decided to do physically what he'd already done mentally. He walked out the room and vanished.

———

Evelyn went outside to look for him, but he was nowhere to be found. She assumed that he was already in a taxi headed back to his hotel room. She tried to call him, but he didn't answer.

As she walked back into the gala, she found herself frustrated and angry. Although she was also surprised to learn of the Nkosis' plural relationship, she felt humiliated by the way Solomon reacted to them. Disturbed and perplexed, she tried calling him again to find out what was going on with him, but again, there was no answer. She decided not to call him anymore. Once the gala ended, she'd just go by his hotel and have a talk with him. Maybe by then, he would have pulled himself together.

Walking back into the affair, she shamefully approached Jonas and his wives.

"I truly apologize for what just happened. I don't know what made Solomon behave that way. In all my time of knowing him, I've never seen him act like that. So please accept my apologies."

"I agree that his reaction was strange, but it's nothing new for us," Jonas responded. "We're accustomed to negative responses when people find out about our marriage, even in our own country. Therefore, we were definitely prepared for people displaying signs of uncomfortableness here in the America, although your Solomon's reaction was different from anything we've ever experienced before. Nevertheless, you don't owe us any apology. We just hope he's all right."

"Thanks for being understanding," she said, feeling a little less ashamed. "Come," she said, motioning to him and his wives. "It's your night to be honored, Jonas."

At her direction, they all went and took their seats, and the program continued as planned. However, throughout the rest of the evening, she couldn't get Solomon's reaction out of her mind.

CHAPTER 15

Throughout his taxi ride back to his room, Solomon had been trying to understand why he reacted to the Nkosis as he did. Jan had called a few times during the taxi ride and again when he got back to the room, but he didn't answer. Finally, he decided it was best to talk to her to alleviate any worries that she might have from her inability to reach him.

"Hi, Jan," he said, somewhat frustrated.

"What's going on? Why aren't you answering my calls?" she inquired angrily.

"Look," he said sternly, "I'm sorry I didn't answer, but I'm just not in the mood for talking."

"Well, what the hell is wrong with you? I'm shocked and bothered by your tone. I don't know what the problem is with you tonight, but it's clear something is vexing you. By the time I call you in the morning, have it worked out."

"Okay," he said, growing more irritated. "Just give me until tomorrow. I'll call you in the morning."

Then he hung up without saying good-bye. He texted Evelyn: *I apologize for my craziness tonight. I'm dealing with something, so please don't come by later. We'll talk tomorrow once I've clear my head.*

He turned off his cell phone, called the hotel operator, and directed that no calls be put through to his room.

As he lay in his bed, the biblical passage about Jacob wrestling with the angel crossed his mind. It was a fitting description of the moment. He was alone and wrestling, but not with an angel. Instead, he was wrestling with himself. He needed to understand why he became rattled by the knowledge that Jonas had two wives.

The room was dark and his mood somber. He sat on the edge of the bed with his face buried in his hands and thought about his embarrassing behavior. He was frustrated with himself and frustrated even more with the entire circumstances his infidelity had spawned. Puzzled by how he'd reacted, he groped through his mind to find a light of clarity—the *why* of his troublesome response to the Nkosis.

Hearing a knock at the door, he begrudgingly got up and peered through the peephole. He saw it was Evelyn.

"Damn," he said, opening the door.

"I told you not to come by and that I would call you tomorrow."

"You did, but I was worried about you. Why do you have the lights off?"

"Because I want them off; it helps me to think," he said angrily.

"You don't have to be angry at me, Solomon. I knew you wouldn't like me coming by, especially after your text, but your behavior distressed me. I haven't seen you respond that way to anything. For me, my concern for you outweighed your expressed desire to be left alone."

He decided to forgo an argument with her about her being there against his request. Instead, he went and sat on the edge of the bed with his arms folded, gazing into the darkness, as she took a seat.

"Why did you respond to the Nkosis the way you did tonight, Solomon?"

"I don't know," he said sharply. "That's what I'm struggling to find out."

Despite her presence, he returned to his efforts to search out the cause of the scene he'd made. As he dissected his thoughts and feelings, he realized that Jonas's announcement that both women were his wives had come as a bombshell to him, a shock to his senses.

"I've known a lot of men who've secretly had more than one woman," he said aloud. "Some of the men I've known have even been in long-term affairs with multiple women at the same time. Yet, in all my living, I've never met a man in an open relationship with two women and definitely not one openly married to them both."

"Are you talking to me or yourself?" she asked, growing evermore frustrated with him.

He didn't respond. Instead, he leaned forward, gripping his head with his hands as his mind transported him back to that awkward moment at the embassy. A speck of lucidness appeared in his mind as he saw how his initial shock had quickly turned into anger. He sat back up. Expanding his clarity in the moment would require being totally and brutally honest with himself.

"Seeing them together just made me angry," he admitted, speaking toward her.

As he thought back to his response to Jan's call, the anger had been evident in his tone.

"Angry about what?" she asked, but he didn't hear her as he was already tunneling deep into his mind for that answer. He lay back against the headboard as he continued to fight with his mind to find an explanation for his anger.

Why did the knowledge of Jonas and his wives enrage me?

He kept up his intense self-interrogation, sorting through layers of denial, resistance, and pretending not to really know, until finally, stripped of all emotional defensiveness, he arrived at another truth.

"I was angry because in that moment I was jealous of Jonas," he admitted to her. Before she could respond, he cut her off. "Don't ask; I know. What was there to be jealous of?"

The wrestling continued.

What reason did I have to feel that way?

Solving that part of the emotional riddle didn't take long.

"It wasn't the mere fact that Jonas was married to those two women that jolted me," he said. "I guess what truly bothered me was the way they all seemed content in their shared relationship. Jonas said, 'They both are,' with such pride," he said with a tone of disdain.

"What's wrong with that?" she asked. "I admit that even for me it was different and kind of strange seeing them together, but it's no different than seeing two men together. Alternative relationships are a fact of life in today's world. If it had been two men or two women displaying affections or openly declaring their love for each other, would you have freaked out? You've certainly become comfortable with those expressions of love and marriage, haven't you?"

He laughed. Then he got up and turned on a lamp. There was no more need for darkness, since the light of truth had shone into his mind.

"Wow!" he yelled. "You're right. I definitely wouldn't have flipped out in those circumstances. It's just that all my life I've been socialized to believe that a man has no right to love more than one woman. Hence, the idea of women sharing a man openly, honestly, and happily was unthinkable. Yet here was a family boldly doing just that. To be truthful, it blew my mind."

He returned to the part of the bed nearest to her chair and sat.

"I guess the real deal, being totally honest, is that I was jealous, because in that moment of seeing a free man, I realized that I'm a caged bird!"

"What does that mean?" she said, perplexed.

"Evelyn, the man who said, 'They both are,' is free to love two women in a way that's respectful to them both. He has no need to hide the affections he has for either of them, nor does he have to lie and sneak around. Instead, Jonas feels dignity and pride about his plural situation, and it showed."

He paused. "In contrast, I've loved you and Jan in a way that has diminished the decency of my actions, and therefore, robbed me of feeling any dignity and joy in what I've been doing. Even though so much seems right about what you and I feel for each other, without a pathway in this world for me to freely and honestly love you and Jan at the same time, I simply fell into a trap like many men before me."

"And what trap is that, may I ask? I'm starting to feel a little uncomfortable about this kind of talk from you."

"With my mind boxed in by a cultural framing that made even the thought of an open and honest sharing between a man and two women out of the question, I could only do what an imprisoned mind often does, which is to act in shameful, harmful, and hurtful ways. That's the trap, or I should say, cage, I was imprisoned in. However, I didn't know I was a caged man until I met a man who was free. Then the revelation hit me, and it made me angry."

Suddenly, he wanted—needed—to know more about the idea of open plural relationships.

"Look, Evelyn, it's late. As I said in the text, I need time to myself to continue to make sense of this evening. I told you I'd call you in the morning once I've worked everything out in my mind. Please go home and give me the space I need right now."

Reluctantly she complied and left.

CHAPTER 16

After Evelyn departed, Solomon took out his computer and started researching relationships where people are openly involved with more than one lover at the same time. The first site he searched was on "polyamory," a broad term for varying scenarios of open and consensual multiple-partner relationships. He was surprised to discover the diversity of multipartner relationships that now existed, reflecting the different values, desires, and choices of people. While many of the types of relationships he found didn't fit his circumstances, the idea behind the concept of polyamory—namely, that it was acceptable for people to consider relationship options that run counter to monogamy, heightened his interest.

Next, his investigation led him to the concept of polygamy. He knew the term from its association with African culture and men having more than one wife. From the research, he now understood that the term referred not just to men with multiple wives but also to women with multiple husbands. He'd never thought about the idea of a woman being married to more than one man at the same time, even though the fact of a woman having an affair with more than one man concurrently was just as common as men who secretly had more than one woman.

His inquiry into polygamous marriages opened to him all the worlds where a woman sharing a husband was a common practice. He was surprised to learn that polygamy was prominent among indigenous societies and that seventy-five percent of all past societies had allowed it. Even the Bible recorded the stories of great men who loved more than one woman. Certainly, among Africans, it was commonplace.

He wondered, given polygamy's prior role and value in past societies, why the idea was now a relic of the past, especially since the acceptance of alternative forms of relationship was becoming widespread. Further study revealed to him that opposition to the practice of polygamy among Western societies emerged in part from a societal need to renounce the cultural practices of people of color as inferior and unacceptable for white society. These cultural prejudices against polygamous families gained a stronghold not only among Westerners but also among those of African descent who lost the link to their own cultural traditions as they became westernized.

Armed with a greater sense of comprehension, he grasped the quagmire he'd gotten himself into through his relationship with Evelyn. *Over the past three years, I've been living a tragedy that plays out every day as men like me, seized by love and passion yet stripped of a cultural practice that could create healthy pathways and spaces to love more than one woman, traveled the dead-end streets by having affairs. Moreover, as we men traveled the path of betraying the love and faith women placed in us, we left casualties along the way.* His involvement in this clandestine affair with Evelyn was evidence of that fact.

He understood now more than before that his affair with Evelyn was wrong because it lacked honesty and openness and it wasn't consensual. He and Evelyn had consented, but Jan was never given the opportunity to agree to be a part of a three-way love affair. In the process, he'd breached Jan's trust and violated his most sacred values.

"Trying to have more than one woman without openness, honesty, and mutual consent by all involved is a mistake committed too often by black men," he uttered with a sigh.

He fell back on his bed, exhausted from the long day and from everything that had unfolded over the past hours. Yet, he was glad he'd met Jonas, and he was glad for the inner turmoil meeting Jonas and his wives had caused him. Before tonight and his encounter with the Nkosis, he'd never questioned the belief that monogamy was the only relationship possibility. However, tonight he'd seen an alternative type of relationship that was shocking but real. Tonight he'd come to see that a man could love two women and have them love him in a healthy way. Jonas, Nandi, and Tabisa had shown him that fact. He uttered aloud a final summation to all the insights the night had brought to him.

"The healthy pathway to a man engaged with more than one woman should only be traveled by people like Jonas, Nandi, and Tabisa, who have the courage to embrace an African way and make it work for them."

A sense of gratitude came upon him as he realized the profound gift that meeting with Jonas's family had given him. These three people from South Africa had blown the bars off his cultural cage, and with those bars shattered, the light of a new possibility shone into his thoughts. They were his emancipators, and he was indebted to them.

He now knew what he wanted to do going forward. He'd found himself, and he was prepared to be true to the self he'd found.

He texted a message to Evelyn: *All is well now. I'll call you tomorrow. Sweet dreams!*

He looked at his watch. It was four in the morning, and he was ready for the needed sleep. He lay on his bed, closed his eyes, and rested peacefully.

CHAPTER 17

A few hours later, Solomon woke. He could hear the birds chirping their presence. He felt like chirping too. First the first time in a long time he felt happy and at peace with the world. Although he'd slept only two hours, he felt refreshed. He'd resolved his inner conflicts and contradictions, and he felt inner peace. His first order of business was to call Jan.

"What the hell was going on with you last night, Solomon?" she barked.

He laughed. "Good morning to you too, Jan!" he said.

"Okay, it's obvious that the old Solomon is back and not the one I talked to last night, the one who wouldn't answer my calls, and when he did, he talked as if he was irritated. Welcome back, old Solomon."

He laughed again. "You're too much! You're right; the person you talked to last night is gone. I apologize for letting him out of my head. I was going through something internally, a struggle within my soul. I'll talk to you about it when I get back this weekend. Just be assured, the person you talked to last night will never show up again."

"Good. I don't like that person. He's too different from the regular, normal Solomon."

"The old, regular Solomon won't be coming back either," he replied. "Look, last night I went through a metamorphosis. There were aspects of myself I didn't like, that I needed to change, for the better of me and us."

"What, you've been born again?" she jested.

"I see you're a comedian this morning." He laughed back. "Yes, I've been born again. Not in a religious way but from one dimension of myself to a higher aspect of me—thinking, perceiving, framing my life, and being."

"Okay, Buddha. I look forward to hearing all about the new you. The old Solomon was fine with me until last night. I loved him fiercely, but I do look forward to learning about this new Solomon, as long as the guy from last night doesn't return."

"He won't; I promise you," he said.

They ended the call. It was the first step of a long journey on the path of freedom. He knew that turmoil waited in the coming days, yet he realized that there could be no birth without contractions.

Afterward, he called Evelyn. He knew she'd be waiting by the phone for his morning call. It was another routine when he was in town. His call was her sunlight, ushering in her new day. He also knew she was anxious about the future of their relationship. Like Jan, she also loved the old Solomon fiercely. However, this morning's call to her wouldn't provide him with enough time to discuss everything they would need to talk about, only the time necessary to give her instructions on his next step.

Evelyn answered the phone. "Are you all right?"

"Actually, I'm great now. I've resolved my struggles from last night and our relationship will be the better for it going forward."

"We're going forward! That's good to hear," she said excited. "I'm relieved."

"I know it's been hard for you dealing with the uncertainty of our relationship," he said. "Trust me; everything is gonna work out."

Before she could respond, he said, "I need a favor. I need you to contact Jonas and set up a time tomorrow evening for me to talk with him and his wives."

"What for Solomon? I don't know if that's a good idea. Remember, you were very disrespectful last night."

"Evelyn, don't think; just make the call. First, I want to apologize face-to-face. Afterward, I have questions about their plural marriage. Talking to them will add to my clarity. Trust me!"

"Okay. It's a risk, but I'll make the call. When can I see you? Can I go with you to the Nkosis?"

"No. You've been patient and understanding all this time. Keep doing that over the next few days, and we will absolutely talk before I leave town on Friday."

———

Jonas, Nandi, and Tabisa couldn't contain their laughter as Solomon took them on a humorous journey of the past twenty-four hours, detailing the emancipation of his soul. They easily accepted his explanation and his apology, understanding the pain a caged bird experiences when he first discovers he's caged. They marveled at his honesty as he openly discussed the past three years, guiding them into the details of his life as if they were reading pages from his diary.

He talked about his marriage and the awesome love he shared with Jan. He discussed meeting Evelyn, resisting their inevitable closeness at first, and then eventually surrendering, his heart being stronger than his head. He talked about his growing love for the two women and the guilt he could never shake. He discussed how this threesome laughing with him tonight had enabled him to confront his cultural paradigm, a culturally created cage. Most importantly, he confessed that now he'd found the opening to a new freedom with all its challenges and possibilities.

In response to his bold honesty, the trio began to walk him through their journey as he'd hoped they would. In fact, it had been his purpose for requesting to meet with them. For two nights, they shared with him all the intimate details of how they managed to become the peculiar family they now were, sparing no details.

At the end of their second night of sharing, he thanked them. The time he'd spent with them invigorated him.

He'd needed these insights into their life as a family, and although he only expected a peek inside, he was happy they'd given him a full tour.

He admired the fact that they lived in a world where two women could embrace each other and declare their love for the same man as he declared his love for them, openly and freely. He understood that his initial response to them was a snapshot of the many moments when they must have encountered negativity from others. Yet, despite whatever resistance they may have encountered, they understood that they didn't need anyone's acceptance to validate the rightness of their three-way marriage. They themselves gave it validation through their mutual love and their pride in the life they'd chosen to live.

Learning how their love started and where it evolved deeply moved him. It gave him hope that he could walk a new path, one with integrity, and a greater alignment with his soul, though that path would be difficult to navigate.

On his way to his room, he thought about going by Evelyn's place before he shut down for the evening, excited about sharing his plan with her. However, he dismissed that thought from his mind. It was late, and he was still tired from the other night's journey into himself. However, he did reach out to Jan before going to bed.

"How's the new Solomon tonight?"

"The new Solomon is doing well."

"Really? How was the visit with the South Africans? Are you thinking about doing business there?"

"The meeting was great. It's all part of the things I want to share with you when I get back."

"Okay, Solomon. Your list of things to share when you return keeps getting bigger, but I'll be patient and wait for this weekend. Don't forget this Friday evening is your men's night out."

"My boys never let me forget that, but thanks for keeping up with it. Talk to you in the morning. I love you."

"I love you too, Solomon."

CHAPTER 18

"Solomon, that idea is crazy," Evelyn barked in a rage. "I knew the reason you wanted to meet with Jonas and his wives was because you were entertaining such an idea. It's totally absurd."

"Why?" he shouted back.

"Because," she yelled, "this is not South Africa; this is America, remember? What you're proposing can't happen here. There're many things acceptable in the good ole USA, but this is definitely on the all-time taboo list."

She started pacing back and forth in obvious distress. She didn't want to lose him, but this proposal was way off the deep end.

"My God, why can't you just let things between us be as they are? I've never pressured you about being married, although it's not my ideal world either, being in love with a married man. Dammit, Solomon, you have the best of all worlds. What man wouldn't want to be in your shoes? You have a wife and a faithful woman on the side, all on your terms and your time, with no demands. I thought that was a man's dream. Why can't you just flow with it? Men have affairs all day in America, from politicians to everyday men. It's as American as apple pie, and there is only one rule to the game: just don't get caught. I know this relationship at times is troubling to your soul. I wish it wasn't, but I know it is. However, my dear Solomon, this idea of yours will never work. Never in a hundred years will it work here in America."

"It will never work in America." He kept repeating her words like a mantra. "Why can't it work? According to you, it's already working. All your girlfriends know I'm married, and all my boys back in Chicago know about us. My friends have never protested against our relationship. Have any of your friends ever said anything to you against being with a married man?"

She looked up at him, and her eyes gave the obvious answer to his question, even though she said nothing.

"I thought so," he said, reading her expression. "Apparently, they haven't. I know what they've been saying to you: 'You go, girl.'"

The slight smile she tried hard to hold back confirmed his truth.

"Screw all this hypocrisy. It's okay for me to love another man, and I can cheat with another woman as long as I don't get caught, but having an open and honest relationship with two women is unacceptable, and not for some moral crap either. Our society has legitimized every form of relationship expression, so there's no moral argument it can make against polygamy that can be justified. Society's rejection of polygamy is a cultural rejection, not a moral one!"

"What the hell are you talking about, Solomon? Even in Africa, nobody wants polygamy," she snapped back.

"You don't know what everyone in Africa wants. However, we do know that since the coming of colonialism and slavery, Western hypocritical values have dominated the world," he retorted, pounding on the table like a preacher trying to save a lost soul.

"This is not some damn civil-rights issue," she yelled. "The social norms and rules that govern society here in America are clear. As I said before, in our society, it's simply taboo for men to have two wives or two women as lovers, openly. Secretly, no problem; openly, no way," she continued shouting.

"Unless," he rebutted, "you're Hugh Hefner or some playboy; then it's okay I guess."

"Solomon!" She was now screaming, out of control. "This is America, a monogamous society. You can't have two women openly, and you damn sure can't be married to two women at the same time. It's frowned upon here."

She plunked down in the chair, pissed, as she stared at him in disgust from having to deal with what she considered an insane idea.

He got quiet and remained silent for a few minutes, pondering everything she'd said and all the emotions that went with it. Then, in a calmer tone, he spoke as she held her head down.

"You're right. Given the context we're in, my idea is way out of the norm."

"That's an understatement," she rebutted in a harsh tone.

He stared back at her, trying not to become riled again. To calm himself he took a few deep breaths and then continued talking.

"Yes, it is a radical idea I admit. Yet my choices are limited. Although you're prepared to remain my lover on the down low, and we probably could continue to make it work, I can't emotionally endure our affair any longer. I'm tired of lying to Jan. I'm just not the type of man who can live his life constantly lying. I've fought and suppressed the guilt all these years, but I can't do it any longer. Can't you understand that?"

"I certainly understand; you know I do, so give me a break with this," she said, frowning again.

"You need to pull it together, Evelyn!" he admonished as she rolled her eyes at him and puckered her lips.

"The way you and I are trying to hold on to each other is not fair to Jan, you, or me. All of this is my fault. I never imagined myself in an affair. It just wasn't an idea I embraced. Nor did I desire someone outside of my marriage. My mistake was creating the space for us to know each other and allowing a love to flourish that had no future possibilities. Before I came to DC this time, I'd already made up my mind to end my trips here and to end my relationship with you. That's what I wanted to talk to you about, which I'm sure you knew. Yet meeting Jonas and his wives put the thought of another way forward on my mind. If I'm going to love two women, then it will have to be an open and honest love. I don't want to end this relationship with you, but if continuing as we've done in the past is the only way to have you in my life and me in yours, then our life together is over. I just can't do us this way anymore," he said emphatically.

Those words caused her to look up at him sadly.

"If you don't think my idea makes sense, I'll not attempt to execute my plan. I'll simply end our relationship as I intended to do. However, I'm still going to tell Jan the truth about us. She deserves that much from me."

"Solomon," she replied, calmer than before, "I acknowledge that you've tried to resist our growing intimacy, and that I offered little resistance, mainly because I'm certain that something deep within our souls brought us together. I've come to love you deeper than I've ever loved any man, and I want to hold on to that love. Therefore, I'll travel with you down any path that will keep us together, because I don't want to live my life without you. If it only depended on me, I'd be all in with this idea of yours. However, do you really think that you're going to be able to tell Jan that for almost three years, you've been having an affair but now you want to come clean? 'Oh, and by the way, Jan, would you agree to share me with my lover, Evelyn, so I can stop feeling bad about loving two women?' If you think Jan is going to accept that, I got a bridge to sell you in Brooklyn."

"I'm not that stupid, Evelyn, and I'm not that naïve," he said sharply. "I know that the chance of getting Jan to forgive my gross violation of our marriage and open herself up to the idea of the three of us existing together is zero."

"Then what's the point? If you know that Jan's never going to accept your confession of love for another woman, and that she's certainly not going to want to share in any kind of tripartite love, what's the point of telling her? I hear you and understand when you say you can't do us this way anymore. I get that. But still, I don't understand why you feel the need to tell her about a relationship you're ending and then discuss this idea of the three of us in an open shared relationship when you already know she'll be totally opposed to it."

"Evelyn, this is about more than getting her to agree to the possibility of the three of us sharing our lives together; it is important for me to restore my integrity."

He began to walk back and forth like an attorney in a courtroom.

"I know this is not the ideal way to bring all of this into the light. However, you and I have already trespassed all the boundaries that would have made another way forward possible."

With that sharp rebuke of their past actions, she was silenced.

"I just got to be honest with Jan now about everything. I got to—in order to restore myself back to the true me. I assure you, I'm not that far off into la-la land. I know that in the pain of my confession, the idea of a shared relationship will anger her even more, but at least the possibility would have been put on the table. If she wants to end our marriage over the revelation of my affair, I'll accept that because what I've done to her is wrong. However, I'm insulted by your attempts to make it seem like I'm totally stupid. Let's not talk any further. I'll be leaving tomorrow evening, going back to Chicago. You're right; my proposal is so farfetched that it can never happen. Therefore, it is very unlikely that I'll be seeing you again."

With those words, he left. She tried to grab him before he got out the door, to keep the dialogue going, but she was unsuccessful.

———

The next day, as he was leaving for the airport, he saw her call on his phone.

"Hi," he answered. "I just left work, and I'm on my way to Reagan."

"I know," she said. "Listen, as I said before, I believe in you, and I believe in us. I never thought there was a possibility of us being more than what we were, but I'm willing to work to make it more. If you believe that such a possibility exists, I'll do whatever it takes on my end. If you can get Jan there, you can count me in."

"As I said yesterday, Evelyn, I'm not trying to get anyone anywhere. I'm just trying to be totally honest with Jan for the first time in three years. Truthfully, as you said, under the circumstances, even holding on to my marriage will be difficult, if not impossible. Anything else is definitely a long shot. However, no matter what happens, at least I can live with myself going forward, whatever the cost. I'm committed to being truthful with Jan about you and me, and I'm committed to affirming to her the value of a plural relationship as one of the options for us, although the time has passed for any real buy-in from her. It's just the right thing for me to do in light of what the Nkosis taught me."

"I understand. I'm sorry for last night's argument and for all the pain this has brought to you."

"It's not your fault, Evelyn. It's my fault entirely, but that's water under the bridge now. We have to move forward and do what's right from this point forward."

"I hear you. You're right. I love you, Solomon!"

"I love you too. Take care of yourself."

"I'll try. When will I talk to you?"

"I can't say for sure, but the first chance I get, I'll call you."

"Okay. Have a safe flight."

"Thanks."

PART FOUR

CHAPTER 19

The flight from Reagan National to Midway Airport was only two hours long; however, Solomon wished it were longer. Although he was prepared to face the consequences of his decision, he was in no hurry to deal with the certain challenges that lay ahead. The perils would commence tonight. The first Friday of every month was men's night out. It was a tradition that went back for years, and even Jan knew it was too sacred for any interference on her part. His four lifelong friends—Tony, Lavon, Ralph, and Dwight—would be there. They'd grown up with him on the West Side.

They all knew about his affair with Evelyn. He'd told them about it at one of their gatherings. They received the information with pats on his back, as if the affair meant he'd successfully completed a rite of passage into real manhood. None of them practiced monogamy. Lavon had lived with his girlfriend, Trina, for nine years but refused to marry her because he couldn't see himself belonging to only one woman. Dwight was married but was involved in two extramarital affairs. Tony was in his fourth marriage; the others dubbed him a serial polygamist. Ralph was in the midst of a divorce and was now living with his new girlfriend.

Until they found out about Evelyn, they'd regarded Solomon as henpecked. They liked Jan and understood why he held her in high esteem, but still couldn't avoid pestering him about being a one-woman man. Once, Dwight asked him, "What man did you know in the old West Side neighborhood with only one woman, Solomon?" He viewed the question as farfetched. He'd grown up around plenty of men who were faithful to their wives and lovers. Nevertheless, he understood Dwight's point: a man in a relationship with more than one woman at the same time was common in the old neighborhood.

After the plane landed, Dwight was there on time to pick him up. This month's outing was at Tony's place. Dwight liked making the airport run because it meant he could get any details of Solomon's trip before the others could, and he was always ready to start his interrogation as soon as Solomon entered the car.

"How was this trip?" Dwight asked.

"Vastly different from any other time," he responded, "but I'm a little tired from the week and the plane ride. Let's hold off on further discussions until later this evening."

With that response, Solomon closed his eyes and laid his head back, pretending to sleep to avoid any further conversation. He knew Dwight would be disappointed at his unwillingness to share but would respect the wall he'd erected in the moment.

After a forty-minute ride, they pulled up to Tony's condo. Everyone was there, and as always, they were happy to see one another. They each felt that it was important for them to stay connected even as they grew older and their lives went through different phases and changes. Solomon was the most beloved of the group, so they greeted him with great affection, and each person asked how Jan and Evelyn were doing.

"They're both fine," he responded.

Poker was the game of the evening, and since Solomon was the master of the game, he always ended up with the most winnings. Thus, everyone was shocked at the amount of money he was losing early on in the evening. He noticed Dwight giving the others a certain look after each of his losses.

After about an hour of playing, his preoccupation with some issue besides poker was too obvious for the others to cast aside.

"What the hell's wrong with you, Solomon?" Tony asked.

"What do you mean?" he replied.

"What do I mean? You've already lost one hundred dollars playing stupid. That's not like you."

"Yeah," echoed Dwight. "From the time I picked you up from the airport, I could tell something real deep was on your mind. We're all friends, and we've always shared our problems with each other. Therefore, be straight with us. What's going on with you?"

"Yeah, right," everyone else said, agreeing with Dwight.

No longer able to drag out what he needed to reveal, he began to share his week's experience in Washington. He told them how he'd reached a point where he in good conscience couldn't continue his affair with Evelyn and how he'd decided that he'd end his relationship with her. He saw their negative reactions to that news, although they said nothing and allowed him to continue.

He disclosed all the details of the event at the Ghanaian consulate and the emotional tailspin he'd gone through upon meeting Jonas and his two wives. He shared his soul's struggle to understand what came over him and his subsequent discovery that he'd been living in a cultural cage that prevented him from considering an open plural relationship with two women as a viable option.

He continued to narrate his conversation with the Nkosis and the way they helped him understand that a man could only love two women by doing things the right way, which meant being honest with each woman and getting a true buy-in from each.

Then finally, he told them that he planned to go to Jan and tell her about his affair and put on the table the option of an open shared relationship between him, her, and Evelyn.

At that point, a protest arose from everyone.

"Hell, no, you won't! You're kidding, right? Are you out of your fucking mind?"

Dwight was the most vocal in his protest. Throwing his cards on the table, he rose from his seat and stepped toward Solomon.

"I understand the idea of you being uncomfortable in an affair, but telling Jan about Evelyn in order to get her to participate in a polygamous relationship with you and your other woman is asinine!" Dwight hollered.

He looked up at Dwight. He'd expected this type of response from them. In fact, it was the reason he'd been reluctant to engage them in this discussion, although he'd known it was unavoidable.

"Back the hell off me, Dwight," he said as he rose to his feet and stared into Dwight's face.

The others pulled Dwight away. They could tolerate disagreement, but as friends, they'd never fought, and the others were not going to let it happen on this night.

"You don't have to hold me," Dwight angrily said to the others. "I'm leaving. This nigger has lost his mind with this crazy idea. He meets an African, and now he thinks he's in Africa and can do what they do in Africa. Your wife and my wife are best friends. The lives of all of our women intersect. If you tell your wife this mess, we will all become suspect with our women. If you don't care about destroying your family, think about the impact you'll have on mine."

Dwight was about to leave, but Lavon stopped him.

"Though we hear your concern, Dwight," Lavon said, "all of us are not in your position. I'm not concerned for myself or for my relationship with Trina since we're not married. However, I'm concerned, Solomon, about what this course of action may do to your relationship with Jan. You and Jan have something special that we all admire."

Lavon looked back at the others, and they nodded. Lavon continued.

"We would hate to see you do anything to destroy something that special. If continuing with Evelyn makes you feel guilty and you want to end your relationship with her, then you should definitely end it and move on."

He again looked back at the others, as if they were the jury he needed to win his case.

"However, if you want to keep both Evelyn and Jan, this is certainly not the way to go about doing that."

"Exactly," Tony seconded. "This is a losing approach, Solomon. This way you'll end up with no one. If your aim is to save your marriage, what you're about to do will certainly not help you achieve that."

Solomon walked toward the window and stared out. After gathering himself, he walked away from the window and turned to Tony to begin his rebuke.

"Tony, you're acting as if you know something about what it takes to save a marriage. You've destroyed three marriages because you're incapable of loving any woman. That's why your women always end up divorcing you."

"Wait a minute," Tony said defensively. "I divorced them; they didn't divorce me."

"And you, Dwight," Solomon said, "claiming that I'm putting your relationship at risk by being honest and up-front with my wife. You put your own relationship at risk by believing that you could have other women on the side without risking any harm to your marriage. Don't you know that these illicit affairs by us black men are a major destabilizer of black families?"

Dwight's eyes were red with anger. However, Solomon wasn't finished.

"Don't make me your scapegoat, Dwight," he scolded. "At some point we have to stop believing this myth that cheating is an acceptable pathway for black men. I don't care how many fathers, uncles, brothers, and friends are engaging in the practice; it's wrong," he yelled.

"What's wrong with black people? When are we going to own up to this world of men with multiple women that is going on every day in front of our eyes and decide that since it's a part of our world, we need to find a decent way to live it out? Wouldn't that be a better option for us than this widespread conspiracy of denial? Certainly, it would. I'll never again feel that what we men are doing now is better than learning to establish open, honest, and consensual relationships with multiple women, as long as we're going to continue to be in the business of having more than one woman. Never!" he shouted.

"Calm down, Solomon," Ralph said. "We hear you. Some of your points are valid. I often thought about taking the path that you're attempting to embark upon. When I started my relationship with Brenda, it turned out to be more than I expected it would be. I loved my wife, Sarah, and there wasn't anything lacking in my relationship with her. However, my relationship with Brenda grew to a point where I could only hear a voice saying I had to choose one of them. I ended up choosing Brenda. Yet even now, I still have strong feelings for Sarah. If I'd even thought of the possibility of working to keep them both, I would have, but that thought never came to my mind. In every situation I've known where men have had more than one woman, they kept one a secret, or they chose between them."

The others nodded in agreement.

"Although what you're saying is intriguing, I don't think it's something you can accomplish among African American women. Among African women, who are exposed to polygamy, it is possible, but the sisters are not going for it, especially Jan."

"Ralph," Solomon said in a calmer tone, "the point is not whether our women will accept being a part of a plural relationship. The point is that we have to act with integrity and give them that choice, and not after we've already gotten involved with someone else, like I'm doing now. No, we must have these buy-in conversations on the front end. Some women will accept it and some will not, and that should be their right. However, it is important that we men free ourselves from this practice of cheating and shift back to an institution from our African past that was taken away by those who didn't want any expressions of Africa maintained. It was their way of saying that everything African, including our marriage systems, was inferior and therefore must be rejected."

He continued. "This is not a truly monogamous society. Instead, it's hypocritical at every point by providing the opportunities for men to engage in illicit affairs. For the sake of our women, our children, and the black community, we must end this hypocrisy. We must either remain faithful to our relationships or find women who will freely and without pressure consent to an open cosharing."

Tony spoke up. "Doing that is only going to encourage our women to advocate for having more than one man."

"Maybe it would, Tony," he responded. "For the women who think they can make that work, honestly and openly, with some men consenting to it, maybe they should have the right to try it. I'm not concerned about that. I'm concerned about all the nonconsensual man-sharing that now exists in our communities and the negative impact it is having on black families. As men, we have to come out of the closet if we truly believe in having more than one woman."

"You do make some sense, Solomon," Lavon admitted, "even though you're now embarking on a path that I don't think none of us could see ourselves walking with you. Nevertheless, you're right. Having an affair is way too much work, which often results in negative consequences for all involved. Yet this idea of overt plural relationships is way over my head."

"See," Dwight said, picking back up his protest. "I told you Solomon is crazy. This crap is not worth us listening to it. Just like I started to do earlier, I'm leaving."

Dwight stepped toward the door again. However, this time Solomon put his arms out and stopped him.

"You don't have to leave, Dwight, because I'm leaving."

"Wait, Solomon." Everyone but Dwight objected. "Don't leave, nor you, Dwight," Ralph said. "We've been friends for a long time, so we can't end the night like this. I may not agree with all you're saying, Solomon, but I respect that it's your decision."

"Thanks, Ralph, and all of you for letting me get this out. It's a lot to digest, I admit, but I'm committed to this path. I have a long day tomorrow. Sharing with Jan will be even more complicated than tonight, so I need to get some sleep."

He put his hands on Dwight's shoulder as he opened the door.

"Thanks for speaking your mind. No hard feelings."

Then he walked out, and Dwight shut the door behind him. He knew that his friendship with the four of them wouldn't be the same going forward.

CHAPTER 20

Solomon entered his condominium, still annoyed by Dwight's line of thinking. The idea that his desire to be truthful to Jan about his extramarital affair could compromise Dwight's cheating lifestyle incensed him, though he was trying to get past it. Discussing everything with Jan tomorrow was the Mount Everest yet to be climbed. Therefore, he didn't want to spend emotional resources focusing on Dwight's self-centered thinking. Instead, he needed to conserve his energy for the more challenging moments ahead.

He arrived home earlier than usual for a men's night out, but there was no sound to indicate that Jan was still awake. He tiptoed about the place, cautious not to wake her, not wanting to explain why he was home early. Moreover, he needed the rest. All he'd been through this week, including the tense moments with the guys, had left him exhausted and desperate for sleep.

He showered, put on a fresh T-shirt and briefs, and quietly eased into bed next to her. He turned on his side away from her and prepared to embrace the sleep his body yearned for. However, his effort to move in stealth failed, as Jan's love sensors, alerted to his presence, aroused her from sleep.

"Ooh, you're home early," she said, sounding pleasantly surprised.

"Yes," he answered. "I was tired from the flight and a long week and I decided to turn in early and get some rest."

She turned toward him and wrapped her arms around him, squeezing him tightly.

"I was just dreaming about you," she said in a sensual whisper. "Now that you're here, I can turn that dream into reality."

She sucked his earlobe, while breathing hard against his neck and pressing her pelvis against him.

"Um, the new Solomon tastes as good as the old one," she said seductively.

She placed her hands under his T-shirt and gently massaged his chest with her smooth hands, rubbing across his well-sculpted pecs and abs. Then she reached down and fondled the outside of his briefs.

He was in a quandary, not knowing how to respond to her obvious intent to make love to him. However, though stimulated, he certainly didn't want to make love to her the night before admitting to his affair.

"Jan, let's postpone this until tomorrow night. It's been a long day for me."

However, his words went unheeded. She turned him around to face her and started sucking his neck softly. Her breath and the moistness of her lips upon his neck caused his head to arch back and his mouth to fall open.

"Oh no, baby," she said in a sultry voice. "I got the hots for you, so sleep is not an option for either of us right now."

With her flames of sexual longings rising, she moved from his neck to his lips. She sucked his top lip and then his bottom, before touching his tongue with hers. Then she sat up and took off her gown. He pulled off his T-shirt and his briefs. Now they were both naked.

He stood over her for a moment, beholding her, his beloved Jan, in all of her beauty, body, and soul.

If I could only undo the last three years, he thought briefly.

She reached up and grabbed his face. Holding his face with both hands, she guided his mouth to one of her breasts. Her nipple hardened as he sucked softly. After a few minutes, she guided him to her other breast.

"Ooh, that's good, Solomon," she whimpered.

As he feasted on her breast, she moved her hips in slow gyration, causing his thigh to press against her pleasure point. He could feel her moisture against his thigh. Excited and no longer reluctant to make love to her, he parted her legs and journeyed inside her.

"Is it as good to the new Solomon as it was to the old one?" she moaned.

"Even better," he whispered.

"Um," she said.

Slowly stroking their hips in coordinated circles, they continued their lovemaking until they both released.

She laughed as she pushed him off her and onto her side, happy and very satisfied.

"Now you can get some rest," she said as she turned on her side away from him.

He lay next to her, thinking, *If this is my last time making love to her, she's certainly given me a night to remember.*

———

By the time he awoke the next morning, she was already gone. He remembered she had to attend a baby shower for one of her coworkers that afternoon; therefore, she was probably out getting a gift. He made himself a bowl of cereal, poured some orange juice, and went to sit down on the balcony.

The lake was in full action. Beach volleyballers were competing, joggers and bikers were in abundance, boats with hoisted sails floated in every direction, and Navy Pier was full, as tourists and others were out experiencing all that was beautiful about lakefront Chicago in the summer.

As he sat there, he thought again, about whether he was taking the right path.

Maybe Evelyn and my friends were right about this being a foolish step on my part.

Then he remembered his night of soul wrestling as he struggled with his past actions in light of the bold life that

Jonas, Nandi, and Tabisa chose to live. He remembered having concluded that either black men must stop cheating or black people needed to reclaim their African custom and make plural relationships an acceptable option. For that to happen, it was essential for men like him to relate to women with integrity and honesty. His resolve returned. He wouldn't turn back now.

CHAPTER 21

Jan came back from the baby shower and saw Solomon sitting on the couch in the family room. Excited, she sat down next to him and laid her hand on his.

"Okay, tell me about all the good stuff you said you'd share with me once you got home."

He pulled his hand from under hers and stood up, rigid, tensed up, and hands slightly trembling. "I don't know where to start, and I guess there's really no best place to start, so I might as well just let it out. I've been romantically involved with a woman in DC for almost three years."

"What?" she said, sitting back against the couch.

She couldn't have heard him right.

"You're kidding, right?" she said, slightly smiling, hoping this was nothing but a poor attempt at making a joke on his part.

He said nothing.

"You're kidding, right?" she asked again, more emphatically. This time her smile was replaced with a frown.

"No, I'm not," he said humbly. "Her name is Evelyn and—"

"Get the hell out, Solomon."

She rose up and pointed toward the door.

"Jan, wait; there's a lot to explain. Give me a chance," he pleaded.

"Hell, no. There's nothing to explain. Just get the hell out of here right now."

He didn't move as she stood there breathing hard, her face contorted by her anger.

"I'm serious, Solomon. You get out of here now."

"Okay, Jan, just let me grab a few things," he said remorsefully.

"No," she hollered. "Don't grab a damn thing; just get the hell out of here."

He stared at her for a minute, and then he left.

———

Devastated by his admission and crying uncontrollably, she immediately picked up the phone and called her mother.

"Hello," Beatrice answered. But Jan couldn't get enough control of herself to start talking.

"Jan, what's wrong?" Beatrice asked, concerned about the way Jan was sobbing.

"Mom," she said, making an effort to tell Beatrice what had just happened.

"Yes, baby, what's wrong?"

"Mom, Solomon had an affair," she finally said.

"Oh, I'm sorry to hear that, baby. Jump in your car and come up here so we can talk."

"Okay, I'm on my way."

She hung up and started gathering some things for the trip knowing that she desperately needed her mother's support to deal with the moment she was now facing.

Three hours later, she pulled into her mother's driveway. Beatrice had been looking out for her and immediately came out to meet her. They embraced on the walkway as she slumped in her mother's arms.

"Mom, I don't know how I'm going to make it through this."

"You'll make it. No matter how hard it seems in moments like this, we women always find a way to get through it. It won't be any different for you. Just come inside, and let's talk about what happened."

Once she settled onto her mother's couch, she shared Solomon's confession.

"I don't understand it. I gave that man the best of me, and then he turned around and cheated on me. What could she possibly have given to him that I wasn't providing already?"

"It's not about that, baby. It's not always about what the woman at home lacks. These things just have a way of happening."

She looked up at her mother. It sounded as if her mother was talking from firsthand experience.

"What did you mean outside when you said we women always find a way to get through this? Were you referring to you and Dad?"

"It happens to women, baby. Lots of women have gone through this. You're not the first, and you won't be the last. You just need to know that. Don't be racking your brains trying to figure out what you didn't do, or whether she's better than you in some way. That line of thinking is a waste of time. Just deal with the reality you're facing, and find a way to move past it. Solomon is a good man who made a mistake. No man is perfect. At some point, you're going to have to forgive him and repair your lives together. The love the two of you share is worth it."

With that statement, Beatrice went into the kitchen to fix Jan some food. "Are you hungry, baby?"

"Mom, I can't eat. I'm too depressed. Also, you can stop that talk of me forgiving him, because I'm never going to forgive him—never."

"You can say what you want to, Jan, and you can let this moment harden your heart, but at some point you're going to have to find the strength to forgive him so that the two of you can move on from this painful moment. At some point, you're going to have to do that. Prolonging the time it takes you to forgive him and move on will only increase your anguish."

She lay down on the couch.

I didn't come here to hear any nonsense about forgiveness. I'm never going to forgive him for this.

Then she drifted off to sleep. When she woke, Beatrice was setting the table. She got up, went into the kitchen, and took a seat, since she was starting to feel a little hungry. Beatrice set the plate of food in front of her and then sat down to her own plate.

"Since it's obvious that Dad cheated on you, how did you handle it?"

Beatrice looked at her and gave a laugh.

"I followed the worn-out path of futility that most women in that situation travel. First, I started trying to figure out where I failed your daddy and what I did to make him take up with someone else. From that dead end, I retreated and took a left turn onto Anger Street. I was talking just as you are now. I swore I didn't want anything to do with him. I was so mad, I went and threw his clothes out on the street and told him not to come to the house again."

Beatrice gave another laugh as she reflected.

"It took me some time to realize that I had three kids who needed their father, and I definitely needed my man, so I had to work through my anger and create a space inside me where he and I could talk in order to work things out and move on with our lives. Raising a family was too important."

"Well, what did Daddy have to say for himself? What was his excuse?"

Beatrice laughed again.

"Jan, you're all book smart, but you got to get some more common sense. Men are no better at explaining how they get caught up in their mess than we women are at trying to figure it out. Sometimes things just happen. People get all caught up in what they're feeling and end up losing their heads. Then they start drifting from the right place, little by little, and before you know it, they're far off track."

She pushed the plate back. She was getting angry at what she felt was her mother's attempt to justify Solomon's actions.

"I didn't come all this way to hear you take his side, Mama. Solomon messed up," she yelled, "and I'm never going to forgive him! I gave him everything, and there's no excuse for his actions."

"Calm down, Jan, and watch yourself. The anger that's building up inside you is going to cost you a lot down the road."

"I don't care what it costs. I'm pissed, and it ain't ever going away. I'm not like you. This is a new day, and we women of today are different from the women of your time. We're not going to take this crap from our men."

She started grabbing her things to leave.

"Where are you going in such a rage?" Beatrice asked.

"I'm sorry, Mom, but we're from a different time, and we think differently about these things. I can't stay and listen to you encourage me to let him off the hook for his cheating by forgiving him."

She walked out, got in the car, and began to drive away. As she looked in her rearview mirror, she saw Beatrice just standing there at the door with her hands on her hips and shaking her head.

CHAPTER 22

A week had passed since Jan's world had descended into turmoil from the knowledge of Solomon's infidelity. To help her deal with the emotional stress she was under, Tasha, Dwight's wife, had orchestrated an afternoon social with her close female friends. After being told of Solomon's affair, Tasha felt it would help Jan to be around the other women to whom she could open up and discuss her marital situation. The others were also eager to get together, having heard that something was going on with Jan's marriage but not knowing the details.

Tasha arrived three hours early to make sure everything was set for the evening, so Jan wouldn't have to trouble herself with any of the preparations. Judging from the stress that showed on Jan's face, it was obvious to Tasha that Jan wasn't winning the emotional struggle this marriage crisis had brought upon her.

"Just relax this evening," she said, squeezing Jan tight.

"Okay, Tasha, I'll do that. Thanks for the support. I need it. It's been a rough week for me. I've stayed home from work the entire week, trying to cope with the hurt and anger I feel inside. Solomon called often, but each time I just refused to answer the phone."

"It's no problem. That's why we have each other, to help one another through moments like this. Just let me get everything ready."

"Fine, I'm going back to lie down. Let me know if you need anything."

"I will. Now go and relax."

Tasha lightly shoved Jan toward her bedroom and diligently went about the business of preparation. The first to arrive after Tasha was Regina, Tony's first wife. She and Tasha were Jan's closest friends, since they both had known her from the beginning of her court-ship with Solomon. They'd grown close because their men were best friends. Following Regina came Trina, Lavon's common-law wife, and Amy and Felicia, who were two of Jan's coworkers. Tasha welcomed each of them.

"Where's Jan? Is she all right?" Regina asked.

"She's resting," Tasha answered. "I'll wake her up soon, and then she can bring us up to date on what's going on. In the meantime, everyone, mingle."

"Great," Regina said. "Lead me to food and wine."

"Right," Trina answered.

The sisters ate and started their chatter. After about an hour of socializing, Jan entered, and everyone smiled and stood to give her an embrace.

Looking at Jan, Regina hollered, "Girl, you look beaten down. We've all been patient, now tell us what's going on."

Tasha was slightly irritated by Regina's lack of tact. Therefore, before Jan could answer, she butted in. "Regina, give Jan time to get something to eat."

"It's no problem, Tasha. I actually feel better talking about it," Jan said.

She took the plate of food Tasha handed to her and sat down with the women.

"Solomon admitted to me that for almost three years he's been in an affair with a woman in Washington. Each month, during his work trips, they've been spending time together."

Tasha looked over at Trina, Amy, and Felicia and saw that they were all shocked to hear that news. Solomon having an affair was probably the last thing they'd expected to hear. Everyone knew that Jan and Solomon held deep affections for each other, and Solomon had never seemed like the type to cheat on his wife. However, Regina displayed no shock at all.

"Is that it?" Regina said, frowning and shrugging her shoulders as if to dismiss the revelation as unworthy of any serious emotional reaction.

"I know you thought your man was perfect and all that, but after all, Jan, he's just a man. Every man cheats at some point in his life. I know we live in America, but, honey, black men got polygamy in their souls. They just can't help themselves. They got to have more than one woman no matter how good we are to them."

"Stop that kind of talk, Regina," Tasha said, in a reprimanding tone. "Jan doesn't need to hear that kind of talk."

"Oh yes, she does," Regina replied, walking about the room with one hand on her hips and her index finger of her other hand pointing in the air.

"The reason she's looking all broken down now is that she really thought her man could be faithful. She really believed he was different from other men. We all know she acted like he was a gift sent down from heaven, but you see, he was just a man after all—a lying, cheating man, like every other man."

Regina's smile suggested she was pleased to hear of Solomon's infidelity.

"That's not right, Regina. I can't believe you're saying this to Jan at a time like this," Tasha said.

"Its fine, Tasha. Let Regina speak her mind," Jan said. "In light of what I'm now facing, Regina's perspective has some value to it. Anyone else have any thoughts on the subject?"

Trina spoke.

"Men do have a tendency to stray from time to time, but I don't see it as negatively as Regina does. I suspect that Lavon has had some affairs, though I can't prove it. However, if he has, he's always come back home to me. That's all that matters, isn't it?"

"Just be quiet, Trina," Regina demanded. "You shouldn't say anything in this moment. You've been with Lavon for nine years and have even given him a son, but he still won't marry you, and we all know the reason why. He simply doesn't want to be legally tied down to one woman, and that's not suspicion; that's a fact!"

Tasha could tell that Trina was hurt by what Regina had to say, especially since Regina was right.

"You're just too much of a coward, Trina, to either make Lavon marry you or move on with your life apart from him."

"Screw you, Regina," Trina belted back at her.

"Wait." Tasha again intervened. "This is not the spirit of our gathering. Regina, we're not here to attack each other. We're here to support Jan. Let's keep our focus."

"I'm not trying to attack anyone," Regina countered. "However, at some point, we women have to stop allowing ourselves to be victimized by our own fanciful ideas regarding our men. That's the only way to help each other in moments like this. Men are known cheaters. That's a fact. That's why I never remarried after Tony. I just didn't want to deal with men's cheating crap anymore. Instead of letting yourself become emotionally crushed, Jan, consider it a blessing that you found out. Let Solomon go, and live your life independent of him, or any man, for that matter. When you need some sex, go and get it from anyone, including another married man, if you have to. Then get back to your independent life."

"That's enough, Regina. If you say any more, I'll put you out of here myself!" Tasha screamed.

"I know you don't want to hear this, Tasha!" Regina screamed back. "Not you, Miss 'Bury Your Head in the Sand like an Ostrich.' I know this is too much for you to handle, since you like to pretend that you don't know Dwight is a whore."

Before Regina could say any more, Tasha slapped her face.

"Whatever he is, Regina, it's none of your damn business. I know you've been bitter all these years from what happened between you and Tony, but don't come here spitting your venom on everyone else. I told you this is not about us; this is about Jan, so cool it."

Regina rubbed her face where Tasha slapped her.

"Okay, Tasha, we've been friends too long to get into a fight tonight. I won't say another word. Jan, I'll continue to share my thoughts with you when we can talk in private."

"No problem, Regina," Jan replied.

Amy asked, "What do you plan to do, Jan? What are your plans going forward?"

"I don't know, Amy. I really don't. My mother thinks that I should forgive Solomon and give him a second chance, but I'm not feeling that right now. What's your advice?"

"I don't have any, since I've never been in this type of situation before. However, there's some merit to your mother's counsel. You know the saying—to err is human and to forgive is divine."

Regina looked over at Amy and shrugged.

"I certainly know the saying, Amy, but like I said, right now I'm not feeling the forgiveness route. I gave Solomon the best of me, and I don't know if I've got it in me to forgive him."

Felicia remained quiet.

"Enough discussing my marital travails; let's play some games and enjoy ourselves," Jan said.

"Good idea," Tasha replied.

They then gathered for a game of Scattergories. Tasha went over to Regina and apologized for slapping her.

"It's okay this time, but don't ever do that again," Regina said sternly.

"I won't," Tasha replied.

After a few hours of fun and fellowship, the gathering ended, and all the women left except Tasha, who stayed behind to help Jan clean up.

"Thanks, Tasha, for making tonight happen. I really needed to spend this time with you all."

"It's really nothing. I know you would do the same for me if the situation were reversed. Listen, I could tell that a lot of what Regina had to say hit home with you, but your world and Regina's are not the same. Yes, she married a man who was no good, but Regina also made mistakes in her marriage. She's spent all this time being bitter, swearing off men, and never owning up to her part. I don't think that approach to life fits you. I can only imagine how painful it was to hear a man like Solomon admit to his mistake, but regardless of what you decide to do, you have to talk with him and come to some decision."

Tasha then hesitated, uncertain if she should tell Jan everything. Then she decided it was best to be totally transparent with her friend.

"Jan, Solomon called me and I talked to him."

"You did?" Jan said, surprised.

"Just once," Tasha admitted. "He called to say he was trying to reach you but that you wouldn't answer his calls. He wanted to know if you were all right. Just talk to him. I'm not going to do like your mother and tell you to forgive him and give him another chance, but please talk to him again, and then make up your mind about what you're going to do."

"You're right. I do need to talk with him. Once he told me about his affair, I went into shock and couldn't bear to spend another second in his presence. I just ordered him to leave immediately. I've been so angry. However, I'm going to follow your advice, talk things out with him, and see where I end up."

"Good," Tasha replied. She then put on her coat and started toward the door.

"Tasha, is it true what Regina said about Dwight?"

"I don't know, Jan. What I do know is that Dwight and I have been together for thirteen years through thick and thin, and for me, that's something to value and hold onto. Good night, Jan."

"Good night, Tasha, and thanks again."

CHAPTER 23

Jan lay in her bed after Tasha left. Angry or not, Tasha was right; she needed to talk to Solomon. Her mother was right too. After a week of being away from him, she was starting to miss him a lot. She reached for her phone and texted him: *I know it's late, but I want you to come over so we can talk.*

He texted her back: *Gladly!*

Anxiously, she went into the bathroom, turned on the shower, and then went to gather a nightgown and robe. She jumped in the shower, washed with a strawberry-scented body wash, came out, dried off, and then applied perfumed lotion all over her body. She thought, *Why am I doing all this preparation?* She knew the answer. Although she was angry with him, she still desired him. She wasn't sure sex would happen, but she wanted to be prepared just in case it got to that point.

Solomon arrived shortly after she'd finished, and they both went into the living room and sat down to talk. He looked as good to her as he had that first day they met at

Bradley, but she didn't want to let on that she was excited to see him. He also looked somewhat worn down, which made her realize how emotionally taxing all of this must have been for him too. She could certainly see the tension on his face and could tell he was nervous.

———

He was indeed nervous. This was new territory for him. Throughout all their years of marriage, they'd never had a serious fight or conflict. Although he was firmly resolved to stay on the path he was taking, he understood that admitting to his relationship with Evelyn had placed him and her on an emotional minefield, which he needed to tread upon carefully.

He inhaled the smell of her perfume and saw the lingerie she was wearing beneath her robe, which increased his uncertainty about her expectations regarding their meeting. While driving over, he'd reaffirmed his intent, which was to finish explaining everything about his relationship with Evelyn. She'd denied him that opportunity when he first confessed to her. However, he hoped that this time she'd hear him out completely regardless of the consequences. He had no expectations or any preconceived ideas about how it would all turn out. He just knew he owed her the absolute truth, and from that truth, she could make up her own mind about what she needed to do next. He inhaled deeply and took his first step.

"You are perfectly justified to be angry at me. However, I regret you didn't give me a chance to share everything with you," he said. However, no sooner than he'd started talking, she unloosed her robe, climbed on his lap, and attempted to kiss him.

Although he was surprised and excited by her actions, he knew having sex would only complicate things. He was sure that what he'd come to share would trigger an emotional outburst from her. Therefore, the moment was too charged for intimacy to happen. Instead, it was best that he continued to bring everything out into the open.

"No, Jan! We can't do this tonight," he said, gently pulling away from her. "We really need to talk things out."

"There's nothing to talk out. I understand what happened," she said.

He was confused by that statement. Uncertain of what she meant and trying to understand the shift in her emotional state from the time he first confessed to her, he inquired, "What is it that you understand?"

"What I understand my dear Solomon is that you were alone in DC for a week each month and a woman obviously pushed herself up on you. Being a man, you found some easy sex you could have while you were away from me, and you succumbed to the temptation. I don't approve of it, and don't ever do it again, but I do understand it. You made a mistake, one that many men have made. I admit I was extremely angry with you in the beginning, but seeing you now helped me realize the importance of our relationship to me. I'm therefore willing to forgive you about this affair. However, I'm disturbed that you would risk destroying our marriage for sex, no matter how good it must have been to you."

Hearing her distorted view of his relationship with Evelyn made him even more certain that emotional perils awaited them, as the truth would shatter her false perception. Still, he took the emotionally painful next step.

"You got it all wrong, Jan. It wasn't like that. That's why we needed to finish talking."

"It wasn't like that. Are you implying that it was about more than sex?" she asked, in a loud tone. The thought seemed to rattle her.

"I was prepared to let go of my anger and move forward with forgiving you under the assumption that your affair was about seduction and sex. Even though it's hard to imagine the man I've known and loved all these years getting involved with another woman for mere sex, it's even harder imagining you having an affair for anything more than sex."

She wrapped her robe back around her and stared fiercely at him.

"All right, tell me what it was about since I seem to have it all wrong."

He took his next step slowly. As his feet touched down, he could feel the trigger of the emotional bomb beneath his feet, but it was too late to avoid the inevitable consequences that awaited his response to her. Nevertheless, he had to say what he'd come to say. She had to know the truth. He inhaled again. He could feel the fear of confrontation coursing throughout his body.

"It certainly wasn't about just sex. We spent time together for almost a year before we actually had sex."

"Don't tell me any more of what it wasn't about," she said in a somber tone. "Tell me what it was about."

He saw her eyes turning red; however, she seemed to be fighting the wrath that was surely gaining strength inside her. He knew his next response would be his final step and that it would drag them into the emotional abyss that they both were trying hard to avoid. He felt sad about having to say what he was about to say. He felt sad for her and for all she'd been to him and meant to him. He wished that he could reverse time and make all of this go away. He wished he'd never started going to DC. Above all, he wished he'd never met Evelyn and found a place in his heart for her in a world where Jan had been the center. He'd wanted to break it off and keep the lie hidden to protect his marriage, but meeting the Nkosis had shattered that plan.

"It was about love," he said, knowing that the words would cause her heart to fall over the cliff and shatter into a thousand pieces. He felt a profound hurt. Not just for her but for all the people like her who loved someone only to have that love violated. He hurt for all that was wrong in a world of cheating men. However, despite her hurt and his, he had to see this through.

"Over the time I spent with Evelyn, I grew fond of her," he agonizingly admitted. "It wasn't just a sexual affair; we loved each other."

He knew that with that admission, there would be no chance at reconciliation going forward. He'd punctured a heart, and the wounds would be too deep for healing to occur anytime soon. Yet, he'd foreseen and reconciled himself to the fate of losing her and the emotional pain it would bring to both of them.

She stood up and started pacing the floor. He'd never seen the fury in her face as he was now seeing, even though she was trying her best to keep the lid on it and let him finish his disclosure.

"You've hurt me deeply, Solomon," she said bitterly, as tears began to fill her eyes. "Although you've done and said all that you can to completely break me down emotionally, I am not going let it happen. I'm gonna bear up at this moment and not surrender myself to this soul-destroying hurt you've brought to me tonight. Even so, I'm aggrieved by your confession of love for another woman. How could you love someone else with all the love I've given to you and all the love the two of us have shared? What need did you have for anyone else's love?"

He offered no answers.

"Obviously, since for some reason you stopped loving me and fell in love with another woman, your purpose in telling me this must be to let me know that you want to leave me for her."

"No, Jan, that's not true. I didn't stop loving you. I love you both—differently but with no less quality of love."

"What the hell are you talking about, Solomon?" she demanded as her simmering rage began to reach a boil.

"I love you both. In the midst of my deep love for you, which has never diminished, I came to love her also. At first, I was uncomfortable with what I was feeling. I hadn't planned to meet someone during my trips and fall in love with them. Yet that's what happened," he said, trying to make sense of something that could never become sensible to her.

"People can't always control love and decide who they'll end up loving. Sometimes, love charts its own path and moves according to its own plans. The more Evelyn and I interacted, the closer we became, and the stronger our attraction to each other became. Before I knew it, she was there in my heart and I felt the love between us growing. Maybe I should've seen it coming from the first time we met in that bar, but I didn't know my heart could be that vulnerable, because I loved you completely. If it were just platonic, it would've never happened. I wasn't desperate for sex; neither did I feel you and I were missing something in our sex life. I just came to love the person she is, and until two weeks ago, I was troubled by the fact of loving her in addition to loving you. I intended to break the relationship off on this last visit to DC until I met the Nkosis."

"What the hell does that have to do with this?" she asked, outraged.

"It has everything to do with it! Until I met the Nkosis, I was still trapped in a cultural cage, not understanding the possibility of a man loving two women without lying."

He began to share his encounter with Jonas and his wives. By that time he'd finished, her rage had boiled over.

"Get to the damn point."

Now tears streamed down her face.

"I'm ready for this damn conversation to end. Spit it out. What's your point in telling me this?"

"I'm telling you this to open your mind up to the full range of possible choices that are now available for you, for us."

"And that's what?" she yelled.

He was now at the end game. The summation of all he'd come to say had arrived. She'd displayed great emotional strength up until this point despite the tears that flowed incessantly from her eyes, yet he knew that with these final words he was about to speak, the space they'd shared together since college would permanently close, and he'd be forced to live in a world without his beloved Jan.

Is there another path?

He thought before he made his next utterances. The answer from his soul was a resounding *no!*

"Obviously, you can end our relationship. However, I certainly hope you won't choose that option, because I love you and I don't want to lose you. Nevertheless, I'd understand it if you made that choice. You can also be angry at me, but give us a second chance, knowing that I'll never engage in a secret affair again."

He paused, needing to take one last breath before he presented the final choice.

"However, there's a third possible choice," he said as he felt a rush of adrenaline increase his heart rate. "Although that choice is difficult to consider in this Western cultural context, it is still no less valid an option for you and for us."

"And what is that option in your mind?" she asked angrily.

"That option is for you to get to know Evelyn better and for the three of us to explore the possibility of a plural relationship."

"That was your plan all along," she said, seething with wrath. "You thought you'd come here, confess your affair, and convince me to agree to your newfound desire to be a polygamist."

"I'm not trying to convince you of anything. I just wanted you to understand all the options that were available to you."

"And you and your damn woman thought there was a chance I'd choose that as an option?"

He could tell she was trying to keep her finger in her emotional dike before the dam broke, and all the anger that was now building up inside her came rushing out.

"To be honest with you, I didn't, and neither did Evelyn. She was happy keeping the relationship where it was, but she understood that the guilt was too much for me, and thus she was prepared to let me go. She felt that putting this option on the table would be a mistake on my part. Even the fellows were against this approach. However, despite their objections, I felt the need for total transparency. I knew that it was highly unlikely you'd consider the option of a plural relationship, but for my own sake, I wanted to put it on the table."

He now moved to bring closure to what he'd come to say.

"I wish this had never happened, and I regret that I descended into a world of deceit and participated in a love triangle without being honest and open with you. I can't take any of it back now, but I can live with my integrity going forward. All the choices are now yours. Whatever you choose, I'll understand and accept."

"I guess that cruise on the Potomac was your little love journey," she snapped.

He didn't answer, but the guilt showed on his face.

"I'm infuriated with you, Solomon. I can't believe that I'm hearing this from you, nor do I recognize this strange man in front of me talking. I only know that my mental health depends on me getting as far away from you as I can. You have become such a liar. You should be ashamed of how far you've fallen from the man you were. As my mother said, you men start drifting from the right place, little by little, and then before you know it, you're lost and can't find your true selves. I should've known you were cheating on me from the little deviations in your behavior that were starting not to add up. I certainly had suspicions. Yet I was blinded to the obvious because I trusted you. Regina was right; we women are stupid for putting so much trust in our men."

Again, he remained silent.

"Thank you for sharing your insanity with me. You will be hearing from my lawyer this week. I don't ever want to see you again, and I damn sure don't want to be in any threesome involving you and your damn mistress. I can't believe you thought that was a real possibility for us. You should've dropped her and kept this whole affair to yourself. No one would've ever known, and I could have continued in the illusion that you were everything I could want in a man. Nevertheless, since you chose full disclosure, live with the consequences of losing a woman who loved you deeper than any woman ever will. Give me your keys, and don't ever call me or come back here again."

He wasn't surprised by her choice. If he'd been in her shoes, he would've made the same choice. However, he was sad. He'd lost a love that could never be replaced, and he would never try to replace her. His justifiable punishment was to live in the emptiness of losing her. He reached in his pocket and handed her the keys, which she snatched from him.

"I perfectly understand, Jan," he said.

"No, the hell you don't!" she screamed back.

Immediately, she ran into his closet and started pulling his clothes off the hangers, ripping and tearing as she went.

"Here, take your damn clothes with you," she said, throwing them at him.

Finally, emotionally spent, she fell upon the pile of rags she'd made and burst into sobbing.

Pained by it all, he walked out.

She was true to her anger and her word. Within two days, he received divorce papers from her lawyer. Within two months, the divorce was final. After a year, not wanting to live in the city without his Jan, he left Chicago to accept a business opportunity in South Africa that Jonas had proposed to him. Prior to leaving, he made a final call to Evelyn. She too had been a victim of his actions and the failure of his willpower. He told her he was relocating to South Africa and asked her to move on with her life and find someone worthy of her love.

PART FIVE

CHAPTER 24

Jan paced back and forth through the apartment, trying to decide whether to make the call. Each day over the past week, she'd gone through this inner struggle. It had been two years since Solomon told her about his affair, causing her to succumb deep into a state of anger. Eventually, she turned to counseling to start the journey of emotional healing. A year ago, her sister married a man who worked at the EPA and moved to DC. Since her sister was starting her second trimester of pregnancy, Jan took a leave of absence to be with her sister until she gave birth.

While rampaging through Solomon's things, she'd found a card for Evelyn's company. Since she was in DC, she wanted to have a woman-to-woman talk with Evelyn, but each time she thought about making the call, she retreated. Finally, determined to overcome her apprehension, she pulled out the card and dialed the number. The phone started ringing, and Evelyn answered.

"Hi, Evelyn, this is Jan Porter. You may not know me, but I'm Solomon's ex-wife. This may seem inappropriate, but I'm in DC, and I would like to meet with you and have a heart-to-heart talk with you."

"You're right, Jan," Evelyn replied. "It's inappropriate, and I'm not going to meet with you, so don't call me again." With that, Evelyn hung up.

———

The call had caught Evelyn by surprise. She was incensed and wondered what Jan expected to accomplish in a face-to-face talk. She certainly wasn't interested in any woman drama related to Solomon since she was still hurting from losing him.

An hour following the call, she looked out her office window and saw a woman looking uptight getting out of a taxi and walking up to the door.

I hope that's not Jan, she thought. *I don't feel like dealing with this shit today.*

She heard the knock on the door and debated whether to answer. Reluctantly she decided to see what this visit was all about. Believing that tact might help defuse a potentially volatile situation, she opened the door and politely introduced herself.

"Hi, I'm Evelyn," she said, reaching out to shake Jan's hand.

Jan ignored the handshake and instead took a seat.

"I guess you're Jan," she said.

"You're damn right I am," Jan answered.

"Look, Jan, I don't want to get caught up in any negative drama."

"You do not have to worry. I'm not here to hurt or harm you. I'm past that part of my anger. However, I do feel you owe it to me to help me understand what occurred between you and Solomon and why it happened, then I can make peace with it all and move on with my life."

Evelyn didn't know what she might be opening herself to, but she agreed to the conversation.

"Okay, let's talk," she said nervously.

Jan took a few minutes and then said, "I want to know why you ruined my marriage and my life."

Evelyn was taken aback by the question.

"Tell me he lied to you and you didn't know he was married. Tell me you wanted to break it off, but he wouldn't let you," Jan demanded.

"I can't tell you any of that."

"Why not?"

"Because it wouldn't be true. I knew he was married the first time we met."

"Then why didn't you leave him alone?" Jan yelled as she stood up. "If you knew he was married, why in hell didn't you leave him alone?"

Evelyn stood up also, not knowing if she would have to defend herself.

"Jan," she hollered back, "you're going to have to control yourself if you really want to have this conversation! I told you I'm not up for drama. Calm down or leave."

"Don't worry about me, dammit. I'm in control. I'm just mad as hell. Answer the question. If he told you he was married, why didn't you leave him alone?" Jan demanded as she sat back down.

What made this woman decide to bother me today? Evelyn pondered. Then she attempted to answer Jan's question.

"I...I couldn't," she stuttered.

"Why the hell not?"

"Because," she said, still hesitating.

"Because what?" Jan yelled.

"Because," she shouted, "Solomon is not the type of man a woman can easily let go of, especially after what I'd been through!"

She started to explain how they met. Sharing that after a long period of mourning her husband's death, she'd gone to the bar as a step toward emotional recovery, found Solomon sitting there, and felt a compelling attraction to him.

"Okay, I get it; you needed to get your life back on track," Jan said, interrupting her. "Hell, I'm trying to do that right now—recover from a great life you helped to screw up. Still, that didn't give you the right to fool around with my man!" Jan shouted.

Evelyn walked over to Jan and pointed her finger.

"Who do you think you are, barging into my office and talking to me like that? You think you have exclusive rights to a man like he's some property you own?" she yelled. "Men like Solomon are rare, and a woman's heart knows something that's true and rare when she experiences it. It was easy to love Solomon. Although I knew his heart was deeply attached to you, I just wanted to occupy whatever part of his world I could. He touched me that deeply," she confessed.

"A woman's heart can't always respect the boundaries that society imposes. I needed a Solomon, a man who could reopen places in my soul that had closed. After finding him, letting him go wasn't an option for me, although I knew he was never totally at peace loving two women."

"Loving two women?" Jan yelled back in a manner that said "this woman is crazy."

"What the hell are you talking about? Solomon didn't love you. You were just some fling he didn't have the courage to break off until it was too late."

"That may be the shit you tell yourself to bring comfort to your mind, but we were certainly more than some fling," she responded. "We spent nearly three years together as lovers; would you call that a fling?"

"Make it be whatever you needed it to be to justify your actions," Jan hollered. "Still, he was my man, and you should've left him alone."

Jan grabbed her purse and stormed out the door to flag down a taxi.

Evelyn ran to the door behind her.

"He was not your possession to keep for yourself! I loved him just as much as you did!" she yelled out.

By the time she finished yelling, Jan was gone. Furious about their exchange, she slammed the door and kicked over an African statue in the room.

Good riddance, she thought.

CHAPTER 25

Jan showed up at Evelyn's office again two weeks later.

"I'd hoped I wouldn't hear from you again," Evelyn said. "Look, Jan, if you want to know what happened and why it happened, I'll tell you. But if you're not open to the truth, then it makes no sense for us to have a conversation that will only lead to a quarrel that I'm not interested in having with you."

Jan calmed her emotions. She certainly didn't want to slip back into the anger it had taken her two years and hours of counseling to overcome. In addition, she did want to know the truth—needed to know the truth.

"Okay, tell me about your relationship with Solomon."

Evelyn began again to recount the when, where, and why of their affair but didn't get very far into the story, as Jan angrily interrupted her no sooner than she'd started.

"I can't believe that you're here trying to justify having an affair with another woman's husband. I understand that you were lonely and needed to open your heart again to someone. Why didn't you just go and find your own man?

You didn't believe you had what it took to find a man of your own?" Jan said sarcastically.

"You can't believe me? I can't believe you. You bring your ass over to my office, asking me to explain why I got involved with Solomon, but refuse to listen to whatever I have to say. You haven't allowed me the chance to tell my side of this. Get the hell out, Jan. Just get the hell out of here right now."

"Yes, I do want to hear your explanations. However, I'm not interested in any bullshitting excuses. Just admit that you lost your husband and didn't feel confident that you could attract another single man, so you decided to fool around with my man."

"Just get the hell out of here, and don't come back. It makes no difference what I have to say, because you have it all figured out in your own mind. Get the hell out of here right now," Evelyn demanded.

"I'll get out, but you can bet that I'll damn sure be back, and I'll keep coming back until you say something honest and truthful."

"No, you're wrong; this is the last time you're bringing your ass back here. If you come back again, I'll call the police on you."

Jan started toward the door. As she opened it, she looked back at Evelyn.

"I'll be back."

CHAPTER 26

Jan came back again just as she promised to do. A part of Evelyn didn't want to continue dealing with Jan and this troublesome issue, but she knew she was partially to blame for the circumstances wherein the two of them found themselves. Therefore, she felt somewhat obligated to try to help Jan deal with the impact of her affair with Solomon, even if the conversations were painful for both of them. Nevertheless, there was a limit to her patience, and Jan was near that limit.

Jan started their interaction this time by apologizing for her behavior at their last encounter and the abrupt ending that had resulted from it.

"I promise this time to exercise self-control and allow you to talk uninterrupted. I do want to hear it all, and I don't want to continue trying to figure it out myself."

Evelyn began to recall again, right up to the point of discussing the first time she made love with Solomon, but Jan abruptly stopped her.

"That's enough," Jan said. "I'm not interested in hearing any more. I'm sorry, but I'm not ready for that part of the story. I'm not able to handle that. To know that Solomon found intimacy with someone other than me is hard for me to deal with. That's the most painful part of this whole ordeal for me. I know I promised not to interrupt you, but stop there please."

At that command, Evelyn stopped talking, and Jan left quickly.

———

More visits by Jan occurred over the next four months, a fact that was wearing Evelyn down emotionally. The futility of their conversations was frustrating to her, since Jan could not bear to hear her talk about a relationship with Solomon that had grown tender and close. Yet, she understood that both she and Jan were attempting to deal with the emotional baggage that two women experience when one woman cheats with the other woman's husband.

Talking about her time with Solomon was as painful for her as it was for Jan. It meant remembering what she'd been trying for two years to forget: a love that was unforgettable. Yet she realized that neither of them could walk away from these painful interactions, though now she wished they could.

Nevertheless, she couldn't take any more of Jan's condemning approach to their talks. She decided that at Jan's next visit, she'd be the attacker.

CHAPTER 27

At the next visit by Jan, Evelyn quickly started on the offensive.

"Let me ask you a question, Jan, since for the past weeks you've forced me to provide you with explanations, none of which have settled your spirit."

Jan looked up at her. "You really have some nerve. However, I'm tired of the stress of these encounters. Go ahead and ask whatever is on your mind."

"I understand that it was hard for you upon first hearing about the relationship between me and Solomon," she started.

"You mean affair?" Jan countered.

"I'm not going there with you, Jan. Been there and done that already."

Evelyn then continued.

"Although it was devastating when you first found out about our affair, to use your words, I'm certain Solomon expressed enough remorse and contrition to warrant forgiveness and a chance for the two of you to work at reconciling.

I know Solomon, the quality of man he is. I know he has, over the years you two were married, provided you with enough love and caring to warrant a second chance, even if he committed an act as hurtful as infidelity."

"And your point is what, Evelyn? Is there a point to all this?" Jan asked impatiently.

"Yes!" Evelyn responded. "My point is that, had you not been callous and unforgiving, you could have given the marriage a chance to mend. For all the two of you had invested, giving your marriage another chance was the only right thing to do. However, you couldn't find it in your hardened heart to try again. Instead, you divorced the best man a woman could ever have. You explain that. With all the counseling support you've received and his willingness to do anything to save the marriage, why in the hell did you throw a good marriage into the trash? I would have given anything to have him, but without you in his life, he could never be satisfied with anyone else."

Jan looked up at Evelyn with a frown.

"I've had enough of these talks with you. The nerve of you, Evelyn! You're such a selfish woman. You and Solomon thought only about yourselves and the things you two needed and wanted and never once considered the impact of your actions on me, because you both are selfish and inconsiderate at the core.

You know nothing of the emotional struggles I've had to overcome since Solomon admitted to his affair with you and the painful divorce I endured. I poured my heart into

Solomon for all those years, and I was crushed by his infidelity. After our breakup, I started feeling that I'd wasted my life investing my heart in him. I wondered how I could've lived all those years under the delusion that he was the right man for me, only to find out he was a liar and a cheat. The more I felt that way, the more I became bitter and resentful toward life, you, and Solomon, and eventually that anger possessed me.

"It took me these two years to understand that sometimes things happen that are unpleasant, and that I had to find the strength to keep on living without anger and without feeling like a victim. My counselor agreed that talking with you might help me resolve my final issues of bitterness and help me move on with my life, whatever that meant. However, my counselor was wrong, because you're too damn selfish and inconsiderate of the feelings of others to understand what you and Solomon did to me, to my life. I'm drained. These talks with you have been a total waste of my time."

Evelyn was quiet. Deep inside she knew Jan was right.

All this time, I've only been thinking of myself and my own feelings. I never thought or cared about Jan's feelings. Solomon cared, and that was the reason our relationship pained him so much. Now I understand why the only way forward for him was to bear responsibility for his actions and tell her the truth. He was right; she was owed that much.

Now Solomon's point was clear to her. Jan was an unwilling victim of their actions. They'd never asked Jan if she was willing to share her man. It had been selfish on their part. Overcome with sincere remorse, she went over to Jan, knelt before her, and clasped Jan's hand.

"Jan, you're right. I was selfish in not considering how my relationship with Solomon would impact you, your marriage, and your life. As you said, I only thought of myself, and I never thought about you. I couldn't say it before, but listening to you, I can better see Solomon and my actions from your side. I know I can't take the pain of it all away, but please know that, in all sincerity, I'm truly sorry for all the pain I caused you. I don't regret falling in love with Solomon. Honestly, I don't. I truly believe it was destiny for us to meet, know each other, and love each other. Yet the way we went about it was wrong, and for that I'm deeply sorry."

Jan placed her arms around Evelyn, hugged her tightly, and began to cry.

"Thank you, thank you Evelyn! I really needed to hear you say that."

Evelyn started crying too. As the dams broke, and tears of reconciliation flowed from them both, the pain from their encounters of the past weeks began to wash away.

CHAPTER 28

Jan made what she felt would be her final visit to Evelyn a week later. Their last encounter had brought the emotional healing and peace she'd sought and needed, and she was ready to move forward with her life. Furthermore, her sister was close to giving birth, and she didn't want to spend any more time away from her.

"I know you're tired of seeing me," she said, upon entering. "However, I promise you this is the last time you'll have to deal with me," she said with a smile.

"I'm happy to see that you're in a different mental and emotional state, and I'm glad that our last sharing helped move you to this clearing, where the air is fresher," Evelyn replied.

"I never gave you a chance to finish sharing the unfolding of your relationship with Solomon. Before now, I didn't have the emotional strength to hear it all. I'm ready now to let you talk without interruption."

Evelyn laughed. "I'm happy to start again."

Beginning where she'd left off the last time, Evelyn revealed the events that led to her first night of making love with Solomon. Leaving out the details, Evelyn admitted that Solomon's lovemaking was the best.

"You're definitely right about that," Jan said.

Evelyn smiled. "I didn't expect you to agree."

"Why not? Ain't no need for me to lie and pretend that's not true."

Evelyn smiled again and then continued.

"From that magical moment of lovemaking, there was no turning back for me. Although Solomon regretted crossing that boundary, I've never regretted loving and making love to him. Even now, I love him and miss him, and it really hurts."

Hearing that made Jan burst into tears, as Evelyn's confession was her own. Even as she'd tried to shut out the truth of her love for Solomon with the anger she'd felt from his betrayal, Evelyn brought her face-to-face with the awareness that she still loved him, and not being with him hurt her too.

Evelyn reached out and hugged her, and they cried together—another moment of affinity.

Recovering, Evelyn continued.

"I knew that when Solomon came to DC the last time, he was going to break it off with me. For me, loving him meant letting him go, knowing that he couldn't deal with the guilt anymore. However, the day he came to town expecting to end our relationship, the unexpected occurred. That's when he met the Nkosis. Meeting them shifted his paradigm."

Evelyn talked about his proposed idea and their argument before he left to return to Chicago.

"I knew his plan wasn't going to work, and your divorcing him attested to the truth of my insight. However, he concluded that he couldn't continue his relationship with two women unless it was an open and honest cosharing, with all parties consenting. Therefore, he was going to tell you the truth, even though he knew it would mean losing you. I told him he was making a mistake, but Solomon is a man of principles, and once he's clear on a principled direction, there's no changing his mind, no matter the cost."

"That's Solomon. That's what I loved about him," Jan admitted. "You asked me why I didn't give the marriage a second chance."

Evelyn looked up at her and waited for the answer.

"It was stupid, I admit," Jan said. "I just couldn't take the fact that I knew he really did love you. If it had been just a sexual fling, I probably would have tried to work it out with him. However, as you and he insisted all along, it was more than that. Therefore, I was jealous of the idea of the two of you sharing a love that I felt was only meant for him and me. The anger I felt from it ate at me like cancer."

They were both quiet for a long time after that admission.

"Have you heard anything from him recently?" Jan asked.

"No, I haven't. I received a call from him two years ago to let me know that he was leaving to go to South Africa," Evelyn responded. "He again apologized for the way things turned out and asked me to let him go emotionally and find someone else, but there's no one else for me. What about you—have you talked to him?"

"No, but truthfully, I miss him too. Sometimes I feel like you, that there's no other man for me either."

They stared at each other again in prolonged silence. Then Jan broke the silence.

"I've been here for almost six months doing nothing but arguing with you and marking time with my sister while we prepare for this baby to be born," she said. "I need a break. What's going on tonight?"

Evelyn grinned. "Bob James is performing at the Blues Alley."

"You've got to be kidding me," Jan said, laughing.

"I'm serious," Evelyn replied, with a look that urged her to say yes.

"Oh, what the hell," she said. "Let's go."

They jumped in Evelyn's car and headed for Blues Alley. It was a wonderful time of laughing and enjoying the concert and each other's company. At the end of the night, Jan received a call from her brother-in-law saying that her sister's water had broken and they were on their way to the hospital.

With excitement and adrenaline flowing, Jan and Evelyn jumped in the car and rushed over to the hospital. As Jan was about to exit the car, she turned to Evelyn and said, "Thanks for the first night of fun I've experienced in a long time."

Evelyn grasped her hand. "I see now why Solomon loved you so much. Again, I'm sorry for everything."

She looked back at Evelyn and said, "Thanks. I'll be in town for a while. Maybe we'll find more time to get to know each other in a positive way."

"I look forward to that," Evelyn responded.

Then Jan rushed into the hospital, excited about the birth and excited about her life.

PART SIX

CHAPTER 29

The sunset is beautiful, Jan thought, while looking out the window of the plane as it slowly descended. In another thirty minutes, she'd be on the ground in Johannesburg. Not knowing what to expect from this trip, she was filled with excitement and trepidation. She'd gotten Jonas's contact number from Evelyn, and eventually she was able to track down Solomon. With her healing complete after four years of being away from him, she was finally ready to see him again—this time, without the emotional volatility she'd displayed in the past.

She'd called him a month ago and told him she was coming to South Africa to visit him. Although he was surprised to hear from her, he told her he'd be delighted to see her.

They'd arranged for her to visit during a time he'd be in town, but after she booked her flight, something came up, and he and Jonas were forced to travel to Kinshasa to address some business matters. Thus, he'd miss the first three days of her visit. The backup plan entailed Nandi and Tabisa retrieving her from the airport and having the honor of being her chaperone for three days. She wasn't, however, thrilled about the prospects of spending time around the two of them.

As she came out of customs and into the main lobby of the airport, she saw the two sister wives waving, elated to see her. Seeing the two of them together and appearing to be happy was weird.

I wonder if they're putting on their best face for me or are they truly happy. Surely two women sharing a husband must experience a lot of problems.

They gave her a big hug and told her again, how glad they were to see her. Afterward, they paid someone to carry her bags, and they all walked to the car. The bag carrier packed her bags in the trunk of a Mercedes, and the three women rode off together.

Since it was night, there wasn't much to observe as they drove from the airport. Therefore, she was forced to give attention to the interactions of her two hosts. They reminded her of her girlfriends back in Chicago—all fun and laughter, except none of her friends would ever be this happy with each other if they were sharing the same man. The sight of them together was already starting to annoy her.

Maybe this trip wasn't a good idea after all.

The first stop was Nandi and Tabisa's house. They wanted to make sure Jan ate after the long flight, so they'd planned an enjoyable sit-down meal for her. It was the right choice, as she was definitely hungry. She sat at the dining-room table and immediately started chomping on everything that was served, and it all tasted good.

Nandi and Tabisa tried to make small talk with her as they ate, but she wasn't in the mood for too much conversation, since she wasn't yet comfortable around them. Just conceptualizing the idea of two women married to the same man was challenging to her. Watching it up close was awkward.

Their lifestyle will have to grow on me.

Funny, she hadn't factored into her plans for this visit having to engage Jonas's wives, although she surmised that they'd become like family to Solomon. Nevertheless, she knew that at some point she'd have to bring herself to accept their polygamous family if she was going to stay in South Africa for the entire month, as she'd planned. For Solomon's sake, she'd have to give them their proper respect. Today, however, she didn't have that level of acceptance.

After dinner, they headed off toward the place where she'd be staying. When she'd asked Solomon about booking a hotel for her, he'd told her not to worry; he'd take care of it. When she followed up with him to see if he'd secured the hotel room, he, again, told her not to worry because it was taken care of.

After a short drive of about twenty minutes, the women came to a villa enclosed by a wall. After Nandi talked through the intercom, the gate opened, she drove in, and the security guard greeted them. The two-story villa was huge, surrounded by a garden of flowers and trees, with a beautiful fountain flowing in the center of the yard. As they pulled to a stop, a man came out to meet them and assist Jan with her bags.

"Wow!" she gasped. "Who in the hell lives here?"

Both Nandi and Tabisa broke into an outburst of laughter. "Solomon does," Nandi answered. "Like many lonely men, all he does is work, and his businesses have been very successful."

The man took her bags and showed her to her room as Nandi and Tabisa drove away. "Hi, my name is Langa, and I help manage the house for Solomon. If you need anything, let me know. Anele is the chef. Are you hungry?"

"No, just tired."

"Okay, but if you're in need of anything call anyone of us on the intercom and let us know. We're here to ensure you enjoy your stay."

"No problem, Langa. If I need anything, I'll certainly let you know. Good night."

"Good night, miss," he said.

"Langa, call me Jan."

He smiled. "Okay."

She opened her bags and began to unpack her things and hang them up in the closet. Opening the closet door, she discovered a huge space filled with colorful clothes.

Oh my God, she thought.

So many clothes filling such a large space revealed a level of extravagance she hadn't seen before. *To whom do all these clothes belong?*

She immediately pressed the intercom and called for Langa to come.

"Yes?" he inquired as he entered the room.

"Langa, whose clothes are these?" she asked pointing to the closet.

"They're yours. Solomon wasn't sure if you knew the right type of clothes to wear this time of year, since our seasons are opposite of yours in America, so he had Nandi and Tabisa purchase a few items for you. I hope they fit your taste."

"A few things! That's the understatement of the year. There's a closet full of clothes in there."

He smiled again. "That's just the way Solomon does things. He wanted to make sure there were enough clothes for you to choose from."

"Well," she said with much delight, "you make sure you tell Solomon that I'm grateful for his thoughtfulness and forever in his debt."

"I'll certainly do that. I'm sure he'll be happy to hear that."

After exhausting herself from trying on various combinations of clothes, she climbed under the floral comforter and lay back on the pillows. Being in his villa gave her a sense of peace and happiness that she hadn't experienced since their breakup. She remembered what Nandi had said about him being lonely. She too had been lonely. She'd tried dating other men over the past year, but none could fill the space in her heart he'd occupied. That was one reason she reached out to him and decided to make this trip.

Another reason was Evelyn. As she lay there in the solace of Solomon's man cave, she realized that only Evelyn, the woman who had been the focus of her ire and scorn, could have helped her cross the bridge from a hurtful past to the bed she was now lying in, and the happiness she was experiencing as she lay there.

Who would have thought that months of contentious conversations, full of angry and bitter feelings, would have carried Evelyn and me to a place where we could truly discover each other and develop warmhearted friendship?

It turned out that her psychotherapist had been right. Evelyn was the final piece to her healing. She'd needed a place where she could vent and release her aggrieved emotions, and since Solomon wasn't there, it only left Evelyn to bear the brunt of her blame and anger. As Evelyn moved from an initial unwillingness to accept any blame for her marital breakup with Solomon and owned up, she was able to purge the final vestiges of anger and embrace the forgiveness she needed for her mental health.

Once she was past her anger toward Solomon, Evelyn kept exhorting her to reach back out to him, claiming that Solomon would be very open to reconciliation. Evelyn continually asserted that regardless of the mistakes he'd made, Jan's relationship with Solomon was redeemable.

Over time, Evelyn's urging her to mend her marriage, along with the hunger in her soul for the man who caused her so much grief, had led her to a place of surrender. She remembered how special a man he really was despite all the wrongs he'd committed. Furthermore, it wouldn't make sense for her to forgive Evelyn and allow Evelyn to become a friend while keeping a wall between her and Solomon.

As she lay back in her bed, she also thought about the wisdom her mother had shared, which had become her final impetus for reaching out to Solomon again.

"Baby, if you only judge a man by his mistakes, what man could ever stand before God? You have to judge a man not just by his mistakes but also by what he learns from his mistakes and what he does afterward. That's how you judge a man, baby; that's how God judges a man. No man can walk this path called life and never take a wrong turn, or never even cause others some pain when he loses his way sometimes. If you gonna love a man, you don't have to justify or overlook his mistakes, but you certainly have to learn how to stand with him as he finds his way out of the darkness and back onto his true path. If you love a man, you owe him that much. If you really love him, you owe it to him to embrace him when he reestablishes his footing."

Mothers truly know best, she thought. *They truly do!*

CHAPTER 30

Having wasted most of the morning resting from the long flight and being treated like royalty by Solomon's team, she was now frantically searching the closet for something appropriate to wear to the fashion show. Today was the main runway event for South Africa Fashion Week, and Nandi and Tabisa would be there to get her in less than two hours.

"Dammit, Solomon," she mumbled to herself. "Why did you have to give me so many clothes to choose from? Dammit," she said again, this time out loud, while laughing. The clothes were all so beautiful; it would be hard for her to make up her mind.

"Anele," she hollered out over the intercom, calling for the chef. Langa heard her and came running.

"Do you need something?" he inquired.

"Yes, I need a woman. There're so many clothes in this closet; I can't even begin to decide what to wear to the fashion show Nandi and Tabisa are taking me to today.

Tabisa said the show is a Who's Who event, and that I should dress to impress. Therefore, send Anele here. I need womanly advice."

Langa smiled. "If I'm not mistaken, an outfit has been selected for you already. Excuse me one second."

Langa left and, within a few minutes, came back with one of the most stunning dress designs she'd ever seen.

"Wow! That dress is for me?"

Langa grinned. "Yes. Is it suitable for you? Does it meet your taste?"

"More than you can imagine. Who chose this dress for me?"

Langa gave her a certain look that indicated the answer without him directly saying anything. She couldn't believe what his face was implying.

"Solomon?" she asked with delight.

He nodded affirmatively.

"Oh my goodness," she said joyously as she held the dress close to her body. "That man is overdoing it."

She was flattered by the care and consideration he was showing to her.

"Wait until I see him; I'm going to give him a piece of my mind. Thanks, Langa. Let me go and get ready. I swear, Solomon puts too much pressure on the heart of a woman," she happily declared as he left the room.

———

Her hosts arrived promptly. Upon seeing her exit the house, they were awestruck by how beautiful she looked in her dress.

"We said dress to impress, but you're going to steal the show with that outfit. You look simply stunning," Tabisa raved.

She was blushing uncontrollably.

"Solomon picked this for me to wear," she said proudly.

"It's a Shweshwe design, one of our traditional South African designs. You're wearing an expensive, classy version of it," Nandi explained.

"I'm afraid to ask you what an outfit like this costs," she responded, still blushing.

"Let me just say this, Jan. For you, Solomon will only offer the best, without a concern for cost," Nandi offered.

She sat back in the seat of the Mercedes as they drove off to the fashion show. Inside she wanted to cry. The thought that she'd let so much time and separation come between her and Solomon over the past four years now saddened her. Her mother had been right from the beginning.

"Sometimes men just lose their way, but that doesn't mean they aren't good men," her mother had said to her. "Look at David; he was a man who managed to touch God's heart. Can you imagine that? Can you imagine a man being so special, he touched God's heart?" her mother asked. "Your Solomon was a good man. You just let your anger blind you to that fact, despite my warning you."

Yes, my beloved Solomon, I once was blind, but now I see.

Suddenly, her sadness turned to joy. She was happy she'd come to her senses, happy she was now here in South Africa, and happy for all the signs that told her he still loved and adored her profoundly, even after all the years that had passed. Her blushing returned and became a fixed expression on her face.

CHAPTER 31

The fashion show had been delightful, and the day spent with Nandi and Tabisa had been extremely gratifying. Still, she recognized how uncomfortable she was with their relationship. Their obvious closeness and fondness for each other was admirable and yet strange to her. She decided that when they got back to Solomon's villa, she'd share her feelings with them. She wanted to get to a different attitude regarding the two of them before Solomon returned.

Once they arrived back, she invited them in, saying she had some things to discuss with them. They took seats in the family room, and Anele brought everyone a glass of wine. They sat back, kicked off their shoes, and enjoyed the taste of their drink.

"To be truthful," Jan started, "I'm a little nervous, but I need to have this conversation with you two about this plural relationship thing. I want to know more about it."

"There's no need to be nervous," Nandi responded. "We figured that you would struggle with seeing our relationship up close, a fact they we even mentioned to Solomon. Our desire to help you become comfortable with us was the reason we encouraged him to allow us to spend some quality time with you before he got back. He agreed."

"Well, since you're willing to help me understand your family better, I'm going to jump right in with my questions. Listen, this whole polygamy thing is new to me, and I've never been exposed to any examples in America. Although I admit that back home there are a lot of men with multiple women, it's not the same as what your family is doing. Therefore, truthfully, I'm challenged trying to understand it."

"We get you," Tabisa responded. "Even here in South Africa where polygamy is legal, it's difficult for people to grasp the way we approach it. Therefore, it only makes sense that coming from a place where polygamy is viewed as taboo, you would struggle trying to understand our family. So go ahead and ask any questions you like."

"Before you answer any questions, I really need to know how this plural marriage even came about."

"No problem," Nandi responded. "We love telling our story."

PART SEVEN

CHAPTER 32

Nandi started as the main narrator. She and Tabisa were both children of unofficial polygamous relationships, as each of their fathers had two wives. Although each spent time with their father and loved him, neither of them got the opportunity to develop a relationship with their other mother or the siblings born from that mother. A fact they both regretted.

Over the years, the two developed casual friendships with men, hoping to find a suitable prospect for marriage, but neither were successful. Nevertheless, they remained open to the possible discovery of Mr. Right. Jonas was the reward for their patience.

Jonas also grew up as part of a polygamous family. His father had a wife and three children in Carletonville, where he worked in the mine. Jonas's mother and her four children lived in Polokwane. Jonas was the oldest. He too never knew any of his siblings from his father's other wife until he later moved to Johannesburg. There he met his youngest half-sister, and they became very close.

After Jonas finished secondary school, he went to the University of Johannesburg, concentrating in business management. Upon graduating, he started a business with an influential African National Congress party member from Polokwane, supplying medical equipment to hospitals and clinics. By the age of twenty-nine, using his business partner's ANC contacts to secure a few lucrative contracts, he developed a successful business and became a member of an emerging class of successful, young, black South Africans.

When Nandi and Jonas first met, he was coming out of an expensive apparel shop for women at the Millennium Mall in Sandton. She was there shopping for a gift for Tabisa's twenty-sixth birthday. Talking on his cell phone as he walked out of the store, and not paying attention to where he was going, he almost walked into her.

"Get off that phone and watch where you're going," she scolded him.

"Oh, you thought stumbling into you was accidental," he responded with a smile.

"I'm certain that it was," she countered, responding to his smile with her own.

"It definitely wasn't accidental. I spotted you through the window and thought, *How can I introduce myself to this beautiful woman?* That's when I decided to pretend I was talking on the phone—didn't see you— and accidentally walked into you. You see how smart I am. It worked, didn't it?"

It really did work. He made her take notice of him. If he was trying to interest her, he succeeded. She was interested.

"Man, what a line," she said. "I'm impressed. Now that you have my attention, what's your next move?" She was in full flirt mode.

"My next move is to have you join me for some food. I'm hungry. One of my favorite restaurants is right here in the mall. Do you have time?"

"Let me get this straight. You want me to totally forget that I came to the mall to buy my best friend a gift for her birthday and hang out with you?" she said, smiling and enjoying a long-overdue interaction with an interesting man.

"Not at all," he said. "We can finish your shopping after we eat. In fact, let's come back to this shop. They have the best clothes for women."

"I'm not interested in shopping at a place where you buy clothes for your wife or woman or whoever you were shopping for," she answered, as a way of searching out his relationship status.

"You're already jealous, and it's just our first date? Wow! I'm not married. I was shopping for my sister," he explained.

She tried hard not to show her delight in hearing that he wasn't married, but she couldn't stop blushing.

"Oh, I didn't know this was our first date. In that case, let's definitely have lunch." *Afterward, take me to your place and make passionate love to me*, she thought to herself.

"What's your name?" she asked.

"Jonas," he answered.

"What's yours?"

"Nandi."

"Okay, Nandi, let's go eat."

Lunch with Jonas was extremely pleasant. Once they finished, he took her back to the store, and they selected a colorful dress for Tabisa. Then he paid for it, never flinching at the expensive price tag. She was awed. Afterward, he asked if she was interested in going for a ride in his convertible Audi A3. It was a nice sunny day, so the thought of a ride thrilled her.

The ride into the outskirts of Johannesburg with the convertible top down, listening to him talk about his life and business while she enjoyed his handsome features, made her spirit soar. She'd only known him for a few hours, but something inside her said *I want to keep this man.*

When the ride ended, he took her back to her car at the mall. She was happy and excited. It was the best time she'd ever spent with a man.

"It was great first date. Is it also going to be our last?" she inquired.

"Certainly not," he said, emphatically. "Here's my card. Call me tomorrow and let me know what time I should pick you up," he ordered.

She liked his take-charge manners.

"Yes, sir," she replied compliantly as she left his car and walked toward her own. She was anxious to go home and tell Tabisa of the gift that God had just introduced to her.

CHAPTER 33

Tabisa changed roles with Nandi and became the oral historian. As Nandi's relationship with Jonas deepened, her friendship with Tabisa frayed. Tabisa was accustomed to her and Nandi spending all their time together. Now, Jonas was the center of Nandi's world. While she was happy that Nandi had found the man she longed for, Tabisa began to feel that because of Jonas, she was losing her best friend.

More than that, she became envious of Nandi. She often spent time with Nandi and Jonas, as Nandi would invite her along on many of their dates—a fact Jonas didn't seem to mind. In the sundry moments of being near Jonas, watching him, and listening to him, she began to develop her own attraction to him. As that attraction grew, she began to wish that Jonas belonged to her instead of Nandi, which led to a growing envy and resentfulness toward Nandi.

After Nandi and Jonas married, the gulf between the two female friends continued to grow. Over time, despite Nandi's attempts to plan opportunities for needed girl time, Tabisa became more distant, until weeks went by without them getting together, except for brief conversations via the phone.

No longer able to tolerate their alienation, Nandi called Tabisa to say they really needed to talk. While she was reluctant, especially since she couldn't put her feelings for Jonas into words, she missed Nandi's friendship and knew it was time for them to mend their relationship.

They met on a Saturday afternoon at her apartment.

"Okay, here we are. What's the reason for this talk?"

"You have been acting distant and strange for a long time, mainly since my relationship with Jonas started. It's time for you to be honest," Nandi said. "Why have you been so distant?"

"You really want to know why?"

"Yes, I do" Nandi said amplifying her voice.

"Okay. I hope you can handle this truth you're desperately seeking to have me share."

With that comment, Tabisa began to make her case for being distant. Her argument centered on the claim that since Nandi's relationship with Jonas started, he occupied all of Nandi's time, leaving very few quality moments for the two of them. Although she was happy Nandi had found Jonas, she was disappointed that Nandi would let a man come between them and their close friendship. In addition, although she appreciated the invitations to join Nandi and Jonas on their outings, it was still a threesome and not the one-on-one quality time she wanted with Nandi.

Conveniently, she left out any mention of her attraction to Jonas and her growing envy.

Hearing her explanation enraged Nandi.

"Don't hand me that," Nandi said, shocking Tabisa by the severity of her response. "I know that my marriage to Jonas has brought changes, but I've tried my best to remain close to you. I love you, and I value our friendship, so don't give me that lame stuff about me putting my man between us. You've been the person drifting away from us, so out with the real truth this time."

Tabisa knew Nandi was right. Their distance was her fault. Yet she couldn't tell Nandi the truth for fearing that it would permanently sever their relationship.

"The truth, Tabisa," Nandi belted out again.

Although she really didn't want to, she realized that for their relationship's sake she needed to comply with Nandi's demand, so in a somber voice, she started her humble admission.

"I'm attracted to Jonas. I've been attracted to him since you two started dating. He's not only everything you've wanted; he's also everything I want. However, you have him and not me, and I found myself becoming increasingly resentful of that fact. Feeling that way, I started pulling back from you and distancing myself. It was wrong Nandi, and I'm sorry for letting this happen."

Nandi got up and grabbed her jacket. "Thanks for finally saying what had already become obvious to me. I sensed that my marriage to Jonas was the cause of the growing distance between us. Next time, instead of being a coward, find the courage to discuss your feelings with me."

With that harsh rebuke, Nandi left.

CHAPTER 34

Nandi continued the story, as Jan listened attentively, appreciative of this time with them.

After her confrontation with Tabisa, Nandi felt relieved. She knew Tabisa liked Jonas, and she'd even tried to tell Jonas of her suspicions, but he dismissed her intuition as imaginary. He thought that it was just a difficult time for Tabisa, being single, working, and managing life on her own.

Nevertheless, her intuition proved to be correct.

Tabisa liked Jonas.

She wasn't surprised. What woman, given the chance to know Jonas, wouldn't be attracted to him? As she thought about the fact that Tabisa didn't have someone like Jonas to love, it began to make her sad. Suddenly, an interesting thought began to form in her mind. It was the obvious answer—the only answer to Tabisa's situation. She needed to discuss this idea with Jonas immediately. She wasn't sure how he'd respond, but she loved Tabisa and wanted her to be happy too, therefore she needed to convince him. She had to!

Once Jonas got home, she shared with him the conversation she'd had with Tabisa. He was shocked to hear of Tabisa's confession, not having any hint of her feelings for him.

"Let's be clear, Nandi," he said. "I haven't done anything to encourage those feelings."

"Oh, Jonas, stop," she said, using her hand as a stop sign. "No one is blaming you. Then again, maybe you are to blame. You cause women to fall in love with you with that smooth style of yours, like you did me," she said, laughing. "Now because of your irresistible charm, Tabisa is caught up in you, too."

He looked at her as if to say "I don't find that amusing at all."

"Okay," she said, noticing the look he gave her. "I was just kidding. Jonas, I need to talk with you. I have an idea how we can help Tabisa, but I need you to promise you won't get mad at me for sharing it with you."

"I won't promise you anything, but go ahead and talk," he said.

"It's going to be hard for Tabisa to find a man she really likes," she started.

"How do you know that?"

"I know because Tabisa and I talked often about the kind of man we wanted, and we share the same desires. I remember how hard it was for me to find someone. That's why I was thrilled to meet you. It's also why I understand her feelings for you. If you were her man and I was the best friend, it would be the same situation in reverse."

"Where are you going with this conversation?" he asked, clearly frustrated.

"Let me get directly to the point since you're impatient today."

"Yes, please do that; get to the point, and I'm not being impatient. It's just that you're obviously beating around the bush. Stop wasting time and say whatever it is you are struggling to say."

"Okay. I think you should marry Tabisa, and the three of us should become one family. We all came from polygamous families and we're all familiar with the concept. The difference is, we could really become one close family and not separate as our fathers did with their multiple wives. There, I said it."

Jonas got up from the table and started walking toward the downstairs family room. He looked back at her. "You've lost your mind," he said and then walked downstairs.

She followed him.

"Is that all you can do, walk away? You can't engage me in a sensible discussion of my idea?"

"I can engage you, but I'm not willing to do that," he said pointedly.

"Why not?"

"Because your proposal makes no sense," he said.

"Why do you feel that way?" she probed.

"I can think of a million reasons why your idea is ludicrous," he replied.

"Okay, let's hear them. Let's hear your million reasons."

"I'm not going to provide you with any reason because I'm never going to do what you're suggesting we do. I'm never going to participate in a polygamous relationship. There's always some women and children left out in that deal, and I don't want any part of it."

Seeing how adamant he was, she decided it was best to drop the discussion.

Two days later however, still troubled by Nandi's proposal, Jonas brought the subject up again himself.

"Nandi, you know how tragic polygamy has been for many people here in South Africa, our own families included. Why would you suggest such an idea?"

She knew he was right; polygamy was often an unpleasant experience for the people involved in it, but she believed that, if engaged in differently, it could have value for some people.

"Jonas, the reason why polygamy has been tragic to use your word, is because most of the time women are not included in the decision to become a polygamous family. The man just goes out and gets another wife without the first wife even knowing about it, let alone consenting to it. However, despite the flaws in the way polygamy is currently practiced, I still believe that it's a sensible option for women in South Africa."

"How so?" he asked, appearing perplexed by her statement. "How can you possibly believe that polygamy could be beneficial to women after all the pain our own mothers have gone through?"

"First," she said, delving deeper into what she saw as polygamy's value, "many women in South Africa are confronting the reality that there is a scarcity of men who are productive breadwinners who can adequately provide for a family. Apartheid left many black South African males poor, unskilled, unemployed, or underemployed, and it is going to take a long time to fix that problem, Jonas, even under majority rule. We all know that. Given that reality, there isn't going to be enough productive men for every available woman to have one of her own any time soon. Wouldn't you agree to that?"

"I have nothing to say to that. Finish sharing your point of view."

"No problem. Because of the shortage of qualified men, some women are going to view someone like you as fair game in the hunt for a man, even if you are married. A lot of women in South Africa are already involved with a married man, and it's not going to stop happening. However, the only answer for women can't be either an affair or a flawed polygamy."

She looked over at him and saw that she was starting to make him think.

"Women need other healthy options. If we women could get over the concept of viewing another woman as a rival, then it would be possible for two women to agree to create a healthy plural situation in this environment where sharing happens all the time anyway. The problem is that men don't provide women with such an option because polygamous men are cowards who don't know how to be up front with their women and get real buy-in from them."

Her diatribe against the old polygamy and her argument for neopolygamy was starting to frighten him, not because it didn't make sense but because it was beginning to sound reasonable.

She started again where she'd left off.

"Let's take me and Tabisa. We're already best friends. Why wouldn't it make sense, if we could get past our insecurities, to share a man we both like? It's a win-win for us both. As working women, we could support the family while providing you with extra hands in the house. Furthermore, if we were living together and raising our children together, none of the children would lose their contact with you, their siblings, or their other mother, like we did."

"Your argument has some soundness to it, I admit. However, you're overlooking a few important considerations."

"Tell me what they are," she inquired.

"Most importantly, I don't have feelings for Tabisa. I've never thought of her as anyone other than our friend. Furthermore, the idea of you and Tabisa peacefully co-existing as sister wives sound like a good fairy tale, but it ignores the emotional challenges women face when they share the same man, not to mention living in the same space with that man."

"Those are both good points," she acknowledged. "Let me start with your second point. You're right that in the beginning there will be emotional challenges for Tabisa and for me. However, I believe that we're the kind of women who can talk and work things out. I also believe that with you as the prize, Tabisa would be willing to try it. This leads me to your other point. I know that right now, you have no feelings for Tabisa beyond those of a friend, and as much as I love her, I would never ask you to take Tabisa for a second wife and not have strong feelings for her. Yet I believe that with time and interactions, you'd come to develop deep feelings for her too. Therefore, I'm asking you to let us start dating her and see how it works out for all of us, including me."

"No matter how sensible this idea seems to you, Nandi, I know firsthand the challenges of polygamy, not only for the women and children involved but also for the men. Polygamy requires a lot from a man emotionally and financially, and I'm not sure if I want to stand up to those challenges and demands."

He thought about it. "Okay," he said. "We can discuss your idea with Tabisa and, if she consents, start the dating process. However, I'm going to establish a set of principles to govern this process and ensure it doesn't get out of control."

"Fair enough," she said, with a big smile. "I can't wait to share the good news with Tabisa."

CHAPTER 35

"Is this a joke?" Tabisa shouted in response to the proposal Nandi presented. "I share my feelings for Jonas with you to clear the air and put our friendship back on the right track, and then you go and share my confession with him and afterward come back here to play on my emotions with this April fool's joke?"

Jonas looked over at Tabisa. "As crazy as this proposal sounds—and I too admit it is pretty outrageous—she's not joking; she's serious."

Tabisa looked at the sincere expression on Jonas's face.

Wow, she thought. *From Jonas's look, I guess Nandi is serious.* Then she broke into laughter.

"Let me get this straight, Jonas. You're telling me that Nandi discussed this idea with you, somehow got you to agree to it, and then brought you along to help sell me on the idea. Girlfriend, you're one powerful woman," she said, reaching out and giving Nandi a high five. Then, no longer angry, she looked at Nandi with a smile and said, "Go ahead, girlfriend; I'm all ears."

"Tabisa, my proposal makes sense, and you know it does. You and I have discussed on numerous occasions the challenges we would have trying to find a suitable husband, particularly with so many men still adversely affected by years of apartheid. We also admitted that despite the flaws in its current practice, women sharing a man who has the emotional and financial resources to love and care for them can be beneficial for the women, the man, and their children. However, for it to work right, we felt there has to be consent by all the adults involved. Furthermore, the women in the relationship had to grow beyond their insecurities. Tabisa, how many times have you said that the thought of you and I sharing someone was exciting?"

Tabisa continued to smile at Nandi. "You present a convincing argument, counselor! Jonas, I see how she won you over to her thinking. Okay, counselor, since you managed to get us three to this point, let me say that truthfully speaking, I've certainly thought about Nandi and me sharing you as a husband, Jonas. Therefore, I won't pretend that I'm not jubilant over your proposal, Nandi, especially since both of you have already agreed to it. So, Nandi, Jonas, what's the next step?"

"Wait," Jonas said. "My consent is conditional."

Tabisa turned to Nandi.

"What?"

"Jonas has agreed in principle to the idea of sharing; however, he doesn't have the feelings for you that you have for him right now. What we've agreed to is for the three of us to go through the process of dating to see if we can find happiness and satisfaction together as a threesome. The process could lead to marriage, but also be clear that at this point, we're promising nothing more than the dating process."

"Fair enough," Tabisa stated. "Now which of you are going to explain this dating process?"

Nandi pointed to Jonas. "He will."

CHAPTER 36

Tabisa was the final narrator. Jonas explained to them the dating process by outlining the principles he felt were important if the three of them were to proceed in a positive manner.

"Remember," he admonished both of them, "while the idea of a plural family is exciting to the two of you, we face potential challenges, especially if we want to avoid the errors and mistakes made by many men and women practicing polygamy here in South Africa." Then he outlined the dos and don'ts.

"First, sometimes we will date as a threesome, and sometimes, Nandi, I'll need to be with Tabisa alone. We need the balance of knowing how the three of us fit together and how Tabisa and I get along with each other when we're one-on-one.

"Second, you both may experience some jealousy in the beginning. However, each woman must assume responsibility for her own feelings and work to resolve any ill feelings that may creep up in the process.

"Third, if problems occur, each person must demonstrate integrity and honesty by expressing their feelings and concerns,

using a positive and constructive approach. Conflicts may occur. However, we must practice constructive conflict resolution.

"Fourth, no sex will occur between Tabisa and me in the beginning, until we're certain and sure that we can develop and maintain a true and lasting love for each other.

"Fifth, any of the three of us can call this process off if we feel it is not working out."

Nandi and Tabisa agreed to his guiding principles. After one year of dating and a year of engagement, Tabisa, Nandi, and Jonas were married in a traditional ceremony back in Durban. Afterward, Tabisa moved in with them.

PART EIGHT

CHAPTER 37

"Wow, what a journey," Jan said as the two wrapped up their tale.

"Remember," Nandi said, laughing, "you were the one who wanted to know how our plural family came about."

"Yeah, you're right, and I'm glad I did. Hearing that story gave me a brand-new perspective on the path that brought the three of you together. Now I can get on with my questions.

"Thanks. I see that you two seem to get along really well. However, sometimes it seems like you get along too well for it to be real. I just can't see two women who share the same man being such good friends."

Tabisa and Nandi looked at each other to see who would be the first to address her question. The nod went to Tabisa.

"It is not unusual for people to have questions about whether the closeness we share is real. Many times people, particularly women, get a downright negative attitude toward us. It's like, 'How dare they share a man and be friends!'"

"Yeah, that's it," she admitted. "That's exactly how I've been feeling since I've been around you two."

"We know," Nandi responded. "We've developed keen sensors to the attitudes in our environment over these years. Thus, we were aware of your feelings."

That statement by Nandi made her feel embarrassed.

"I apologize for feeling that way without talking to the two of you," she said.

"You don't owe us an apology," Tabisa said, chiming back in. "We're not intimidated by how others view us. We're very proud of our family and the life we live together. Now back to your question. Are we truly friends, even as we share the same man, or are we just putting on a front for others like you? To be truthful, Jan, we really hate each other," Tabisa said with a smirk.

Jan's mouth dropped wide open.

Nandi fell out laughing. "Tabisa stop trying to be a comedian."

"Just kidding, Jan," Tabisa said, laughing also. "We're definitely friends—best friends. We'd already established an endearing bond before Nandi first met Jonas and introduced him to me."

Tabisa began to explain that she and Nandi grew up together in the same part of Durban, South Africa, and became close friends at the beginning of noncompulsory secondary school. Over time, their friendship grew to the bond of true sisterhood. After graduation, Nandi moved to Johannesburg to stay with her cousin and look for a job. Once she found employment, she sent for Tabisa to join her. Once they both had jobs, they moved into an apartment together until Nandi met and married Jonas.

"So, you see, we've been good friends long before Jonas came along. However, even if we had come to know each other through our love for Jonas, it still would've been necessary for us to establish our own bond. It's not enough for two women to be together just for the man's sake," Tabisa explained.

"We can assure you, that approach to plural relationships will never work," Nandi was quick to add.

"Why not?" Jan asked.

"Because," Tabisa answered, "I didn't just marry Jonas, I married Nandi too, which means Nandi and I must have a healthy relationship with each other also. Without developing our own friendship, over time, the lack of quality in our relationship would pull at the stability of our family."

"Got your point," Jan said. I'm clear that since you two knew each other and were already best friends, it created an easier path for the two of you to share Jonas and find comfort in doing so. But are you saying that since the two of you were already friends, this situation does not present any challenges to the two of you?"

"No, that's not what we're saying," Nandi replied. "In the beginning, we had a lot of problems."

"What type of problems?" she inquired.

"Jealousy problems, mostly," Tabisa answered. "Like many novel ideas, things started smoothly in the beginning; however, as time passed, the problems Jonas had anticipated began to occur. First, Nandi started feeling uncomfortable with me and Jonas displaying outward affections, such as holding hands, hugging, and occasionally kissing."

"That's true," Nandi admitted. "Amazingly, at times I found myself angry with Jonas and Tabisa. It felt as if Jonas was cheating on me. From there I began to feel that Tabisa had manipulated me into making the proposal to share Jonas with her. However, despite what I was feeling at the time, I stuck to the guiding principles, honestly shared my feelings with the other two, and worked internally to put my mind and emotions in the right place."

"Also, as my emotional ties with Jonas grew stronger, I began to feel that because Nandi was the first wife, when we all got married Nandi would get more of Jonas's time and attention. I then went and complained to Jonas that the amount of time he spent between Nandi and me wasn't equal and asked if it was always going to be that way. He responded by explaining to both of us that if we were going to use a measuring cup to judge who was getting the most time and attention, the process couldn't go any further. He said we'd simply have to trust him to love us equally and fairly. He made sense, so we both complied," Tabisa said.

"Wow! It's just like I thought," Jan responded. "Sharing a man does create a lot of problems for the women involved."

"Wait a minute, Jan; you're not hearing us right," Nandi responded. "Sharing Jonas didn't create the jealousy and insecurity issues we experienced; it only triggered them. The root of our problems was really our world view."

"What do you mean by that?" Jan asked.

"Look, many of us grow up believing that the person we love is all ours and ours alone," Nandi said. "So any time I saw Tabisa with Jonas, I struggled with resentment. In those moments, my mind would say, *How dare she kiss my man?*"

"Yes, and even though Jonas was with Nandi before he was with me," Tabisa added, "it still didn't stop me from feeling like his being with her wasn't right. I wanted his love exclusively. Therefore, that need for exclusivity was the root of our challenges," Tabisa declared.

"Keep talking," Jan said, seeking further clarification.

"We've been wrongly taught that love has to be exclusive in order for it to be true love," Nandi said. "However, that's a flawed belief that limits the ability of women to share a man in a healthy way. If we bring that belief into a sharing reality, it won't fit and we'll end up creating problems in the family."

"We're not suggesting that two people cannot agree to have an exclusive commitment to each other and be held accountable for honoring and respecting that commitment," Tabisa added. "We certainly don't condone what Solomon did and what other men have done, which is to entice women under the expectation of having an exclusive relationship and then violate that relationship by cheating on their women."

"We certainly don't," Nandi echoed.

Jan was pleased to hear them say that.

"Let me see if I understand what you're saying. It's wrong to believe that a person, man or woman, can only love you if they don't love anyone else but you."

"That's exactly what we're saying," Tabisa said, smiling. "That's like saying a parent can only love one child at a time. Does that make sense?"

"No, it doesn't," Jan responded.

Tabisa continued. "Though Jonas was trying his best to show us both the love he had for us, we were still operating on the belief that any love he showed toward one of us meant he loved the other one less. That belief then led to feelings of insecurity, jealousy, and resentment toward Jonas and each other."

"Now I get that," she said. "Let's take me for example. I was prepared to accept the fact that Solomon cheated on me for sex away from home, but when he told me it wasn't about sex, it was about love, I went into a depth of anger, and it took me years to climb out of that hole. I just felt rejected. If he loved her, it meant he couldn't have loved me, and that made me mad. I felt like I'd spent all those years giving myself to him, only to have him stop loving me and start loving someone else. He told me that wasn't the case, but I was too angry to understand."

"Exactly," Tabisa said, starting to back up. "Exclusivity can be agreed upon by two people who are seeking exclusivity, but the belief that we're only capable of loving one person at a time is a fallacy that will only damage a shared relationship. Therefore, we had to change our thinking to make our plural relationship work. Once we did that, the quality of our shared relationship improved. From time to time, we got caught up again in the exclusivity falsehood, and problems naturally would occur. The solution was always for us to return back to understanding that Jonas's love for Nandi didn't diminish the quality of his love for me."

"Okay, I agree that a person is capable of loving two people," Jan admitted. "I get that. What do the two of you get from sharing?" she asked. "The benefit for Solomon having two women is obvious. He gets all the goodies."

"To begin with, Jan, having two women is not all that it's dramatized to be for a man," Nandi stated. "It's hard work, keeping two women happy and addressing their mental, emotional, and material needs. Even the ability to have sex with more than one woman does not make polygamy a blissful life for a man. Jonas came from a polygamous family, and he knew the challenges it posed to men. That's why I had to sell him on the idea. Any man jumping up and down about having more than one wife just for the sex really doesn't get it."

"Speaking of sex how does that work?" Jan asked.

"That's a discussion for another time," Nandi responded.

"All right, I'll anxiously wait on the answers to my sex questions."

"Getting back to your first question, a plural family offers a great deal for women," Nandi told her. "Many of our men are still mentally, socially, and economically suffering from years of apartheid. Thus, sharing allowed Tabisa and me to have access to a great man—his spirit, mind, leadership, and wealth. Instead of competing in the down-low market for the same man, as a lot of women are already doing, we're better off openly sharing and creating rules for a healthy engagement. Of course, there are other benefits that we will share as we continue to talk."

"What's your other question?" Tabisa asked. "I'm starting to get tired."

"Okay. Since two people are capable of loving more than one person, why can't the two of you have another man?" Jan asked.

Tabisa smiled. "We always get that question from women. We have no problem with two men sharing a woman. However, we're not interested in having another husband. Our covenant with Jonas wasn't to have a relationship where everyone is free to have other lovers. We're content with Jonas as our only man. We want to be exclusive to him. However, if there are women and men who are capable of being in that type of situation and experiencing it in a healthy way, more power to them. We simply believe that whatever the terms are, they should be worked out up front so everyone can consent to whichever way they want to live. That's where Solomon made his mistake. He didn't get any buy-in from you up front; he just dragged you into an affair you never agreed to be a part of."

"Yeah, you're right. Don't remind me. It may bring on my anger again."

"Don't do that, Jan," Tabisa said, with a laugh. "Solomon understands his mistake, and he'd never do that again. His own integrity won't allow it."

Jan was happy to hear Tabisa affirm the change in Solomon again. "I believe you, Tabisa."

"Would you want to have two husbands, Jan?" Nandi asked.

"Absolutely not," Jan answered. "Solomon is enough man for me."

"That's interesting," Nandi said. "We're always being asked by women, 'If it's all right for women to share a man, is it equally acceptable for men to share a woman?' But when we ask them whether they want to have more than one husband, most answer the same way you do."

"I guess women just need to know the terms are equal," Jan replied.

"I get it," Nandi responded. "The key is for everyone to honestly negotiate the terms up front. I'm sure there's someone on earth for any terms a person may be seeking. Our focus, however, is on the world of men in secret relationships with multiple women and how to bring credibility to a custom that's as old as civilization and a practice that is still common everywhere."

"I understand," Jan said. "Thanks to the both of you for sharing honestly with me, and thanks for a great day. I look forward to talking with you more."

"Thank you for being open to our unique point of view," Nandi said. "There's still one more day before Solomon and Jonas return. Why don't you come over tomorrow and spend the day with us? We can finish answering all your questions, including the sex question, then."

"You got a deal, Nandi," Jan said excitedly.

CHAPTER 38

Jan arrived early the next morning for her second session on polygamy. "You both know that I'm eager to ask the sex questions," she said.

"Yeah, we know. That's always the question in the back of most women's mind when it comes to plural marriages. They all want to know how the sex works," Nandi responded.

"Exactly," Jan said. "How does it work?"

Nandi and Tabisa looked at each other in amazement. "I think we women are too preoccupied with sex in our heads," Nandi said. "However, before I answer your question, let me ask you a question, if you don't mind being honest."

"Go ahead and ask."

"How many times have you had sex with a man over the past four years since you broke up with Solomon? Trust me; it's not a question to trap you in any way. I just want to make a point."

"None," she answered.

"Did that make your life substantially less because of it? Obviously, you didn't die from the lack of sex," Nandi said in jest.

"Well, I must admit that from time to time, I had to get busy with my toys to get some release," Jan countered.

"Okay, we understand that. How often did you feel the urge to do that?"

"Maybe, at the most, once a week," Jan responded.

"So if the right opportunities came your way, you maybe would have enjoyed more sex, but it's safe to say that fifty-two times a year at a minimum was enough to keep you sexually satisfied, right?" Nandi asked.

"You're right, counselor," Jan answered with a smile.

Tabisa had to laugh at that response. "Girl, you're making the lawyer in my sister come out," she said.

"Forget, you both," Nandi said. "Thanks for your honesty, Jan. Most women act as if they're getting sex every day, all day, and thus there's no room for their man to provide sexual satisfaction to anyone else. However, truthfully that's not the case. Very few women have sex more than eight times a month, even in monogamy. That's a fact. Do Nandi and I experience sexual pleasures more than fifty-two times per year or an average of four or more times per month?"

"We certainly do," Tabisa interjected.

"You two are funny," Jan said.

"Tabisa, stop butting into my argument."

"Yes, counselor!"

"My point is that there's enough sex in a plural relationship to keep us women as sexually satisfied as we would be in any monogamous relationship, and in some cases more than that. It's just a matter of how the sexual time is structured in a plural situation. That's different for each family."

"Okay. To summarize, your point is that your sex lives have not been diminished by sharing the same man. I guess there are so many women with no man that whatever sex time they received in sharing a man would be a plus," Jan said.

"You're absolutely right," Tabisa said, with a wink.

———

Their talks continued throughout the day, interspersed with food and wine. Through her varied conversations with these two phenomenal women, Jan gained a deeper appreciation of her hosts. They explained that their aim wasn't to sell the idea of a plural family to her or anyone else. They understood the way of life they'd chosen and its value to them. They only wanted to provide her with an intimate view into another world. Their effort to do that was certainly successful. Now she understood why meeting them had profoundly affected Solomon the way it did and the choices he subsequently made. She was happy to know them and thankful for a glimpse into the beautiful life they'd fashioned as a family.

PART NINE

CHAPTER 39

At the villa, Jan waited anxiously for Solomon's arrival. He'd returned to Johannesburg in the early afternoon, but true to the workaholic he'd become, he'd gone straight into his office. They talked twice by phone, and he told her he looked forward to having dinner with her later at the house, as he'd instructed Anele to prepare something extra delicious for the two of them.

When he mentioned that he was going home to change first, Jan was somewhat confused.

"I thought you lived here at the villa where I'm staying," she said.

"I do live there," he responded, with a laugh. "It's just that the villa is a little far out from town, so I purchased a smaller place closer to downtown for those times when I don't feel like driving that far back, especially when I'm at late meetings that include drinking."

"Does that mean you aren't staying at the villa during my time here?"

"I wasn't planning on it. It's been a long time since we've seen each other and interacted. I wasn't sure how comfortable you'd be with me staying at the villa while you were there."

"Quite comfortable," she responded emphatically. "Actually, I'm a little disappointed. I was looking forward to being near you here. As you said, it's been a long time since we've been in each other's presence."

"That's good to know, Jan, but for now, let's keep it like it is."

"No problem, Solomon. Just know that it's not my desire for you to stay anywhere else but here in the villa while I'm in town."

"Duly noted," he responded.

"I look forward to seeing you later then, for dinner," she said with excitement.

"Me too! I'm thrilled at the thought of it."

Once they finished talking, she thought about him wanting them to take it slow.

He's right. It has been a long time. We both need to take our time, talk things out, and at least reestablish a friendship. Then we could see what else is possible for the two of us. The old relationship we had ended, and the people we were in the past have undergone changes. If there is to be a future for us, then we'll have to start again to build something new. We'll have to learn each other and get to know each other all over again.

She looked down at her watch. If he were anything like the old Solomon, he'd be there within a few minutes.

Sure enough, she soon heard Langa's voice greeting him outside.

It's good to know some things about him haven't changed.

Solomon entered the family room bearing a bright smile. His handsome features were accentuated by the beautiful blue Nehru suit he was wearing. From his sculpted physique, she could tell he'd been keeping himself fit. At the sight of him, feelings that had been long dormant quickened inside her.

Maybe it hasn't been that long after all, she thought. *Some feelings even time can't diminish.*

She smiled back and rose to embrace him, wrapping her arms around him tightly and securely. As she held him her heart overcame anger-induced amnesia, and she remembered all that she'd felt for him over the years they'd loved each other. She thought of their lives together, the day they met at Bradley, all the joys of their eleven years of marriage, the night that he told her of his infidelity, the explosion of anger that pushed her into bitterness and divorce, and their years of separation. She realized that throughout all that had occurred over the past four years, her heart had held on to him, and like she was doing now, refused to let him go.

She continued to cling to him tightly, without words, without explanations, without clarifications, as seconds folded into minutes.

Sometimes the heart just knows, just understands. Words are not needed. Words just get in the way, she thought. *Tonight is one of those times.*

However, despite all the good she felt wrapped in his embrace, thoughts of his unfaithfulness began to seep into her mind again, causing her to pull away from their intimate embrace.

"I'm sorry, Solomon; it's been a long journey and a lot for me to deal with. As much as I enjoy being in your arms right now, it's causing me to feel a lot of different emotions that I need to sort out. Please give me until tomorrow to pull myself together."

"I understand, Jan. As you said, we've been through a lot, especially you. Take your time. I'm not trying to rush anything with you."

"I know you're not, and I don't feel under any pressure; neither do I regret showing you how much I missed you. Just give me until tomorrow to put all of my feelings in their proper place."

"Sure! Do you want Anele to get any food for you?"

"No, I'm fine. I'm just going to lie back and reflect."

"Okay. Have a peaceful rest."

"Thanks, Solomon."

Once he left, she went back to her room and lay on her stomach across the bed. She thought about the host of feelings that overcame her as she held him affectionately, mainly the negative ones. She thought she had fully put the past behind her and was ready to move forward with him to restore their relationship, but obviously, there were still some negative feelings left behind. She remembered her mother's wisdom about forgiveness and letting go of people's past mistakes, especially when they've done all they could to make amends. She therefore, renewed her commitment to follow her heart and not let Solomon's past mistakes interfere with the chance they now have to start anew.

Lying there, she also thought of another feeling that grabbed her while they embraced: horniness. She blushed at the thought of how aroused she felt while enveloped in his arms.

The next time I see him, I am going to strip my clothes off right there and make him give me some, she thought, blushing.

The next morning she reached out to Solomon. "My mind is clear, so it's full speed ahead with wherever this time together takes us."

"I'm all in on that deal too, Jan."

She began to feel like a little girl in love for the first time.

"Would you like to go with me to a soccer match today?"

"Absolutely I would," she answered.

"Okay, I'll pick you up at four."

"I'll be ready.

———

Full of excitement after attending the soccer match together, instead of sitting in the family room to talk, he lifted her and carried her into his bedroom. She was shocked but thrilled to lie in his arms and feel him next to her. She'd desired the moment since she arrived. Before she could tell him how happy she was to be close to him again, he grabbed her and kissed her. Although he was a powerful lover, she'd never seen him exhibit that level of spontaneous and assertive passion.

After a few minutes of intense kissing, he gently pushed her onto the bed and led them on a retreat into indulgences that she'd surely missed over the past years without him, with a sexual intensity she'd never before experienced with him.

Oh my God, she thought as she drifted into a trance-like zone from his rapid and deep journeying within her. She also thought that if he didn't stop soon, she was going to blink out. He must have sensed her thoughts because he stopped as abruptly as he started.

She grabbed him and held him close.

"What was that about?" she asked with a smile. "It's like you were trying to kill me through an overdose of pleasure?" She laughed, still trying to catch her breath.

"It's just an exciting time for me, Jan. I never thought I would have this moment with you again. I thought I had lost you forever. Yet here we are, impassioned like the years apart never happened. It's got me feeling optimistic about the future and about us," he said.

"I hear that, but take it easy on a girl. You know I'm out of shape from the lack of practice. Start slowly, and work your way up to that type of intensity the next time."

They both laughed.

"Okay, my apologies," he said.

"Apologies accepted," she replied.

CHAPTER 40

Solomon had been eager for them to take a ride outside of the city. He wanted her to see the beauty of South Africa, and they needed a time for talking. She agreed. Since he'd returned from Kinshasa, their time together had been a whirlwind of busyness. Although it was fun getting reacquainted, if their goal was to build a foundation for restoring their relationship, they had a lot more to talk about.

He had Anele prepare a picnic basket, and they headed off into the countryside. It was a perfect day for riding. The rolling hills of green were awesomely beautiful, and the wind blowing through their hair was thrilling. More than that, sitting in the space next to her gave him a new joy for living, as the despair of the past faded into the distance behind them.

After two hours of cruising, he parked near a lake, and they got out and spread a blanket on a cool spot of grass under a tree. Jan unpacked some of the food Anele had prepared, and they began to munch on the food while sipping a glass of wine. When they were fully feasted, he rested his head on her lap and stared up into a clear blue sky.

"I often think back to that time of our breakup and all the things I did wrong," he said.

"We don't have to go there, Solomon. I've worked hard to put everything that happened and the emotional scars that came with it behind me so I could get to this space where we could reconnect. I don't know if rehashing it will be good for me."

"I understand, but please let me share my feelings with you. I've waited a long time for this opportunity. I need to do this to clear a space for me to move forward with us."

"Okay, Solomon, I'm all ears."

"I had to understand what was happening inside of me that became the catalyst for my actions. My behavior became inconsistent with the person I'd been prior to meeting Evelyn."

"I agree. That's what was shocking to me also. The Solomon I'd known was a man of integrity. Therefore, I was heartbroken to find out that I didn't know you as much as I thought I did."

"I didn't know me as much as I thought I did either, Jan."

"What do you mean by that?"

"There're layers to a person, and not everything about someone is visible even to themselves. I know now that much of who we are often remains submerged and hidden from our consciousness."

"I agree Solomon. We go through life not knowing everything we need to know about ourselves. However, what does that have to do with you and what occurred?"

"It had a lot to do with what happened! You see, there were empty places in me crying out to be filled, but those cries I muted and muffled without knowing it. It had nothing to do with you. You were everything I could've ever wanted in a woman, and I found delight and satisfaction at the very thought of being with you. However, there were still issues about losing my mother that I never resolved."

"What issues?"

"I underestimated the emotional scars that losing my mother left in me. It wasn't apparent to me in the same way that the emotional effect of losing your father was to you. I should've gotten counseling at the time it happened, to explore my feelings, but I didn't. I simply did what men often do: bury the hurt deep inside and pretend that all is well."

"Yes, a lot of men make that mistake."

"We do. Unfortunately, on the surface, it looked and felt like that approach was working well for me. I was happy as far as I knew. Yet seeing Evelyn, and her resemblance to my mother, unlocked a secret chamber of longings that drew me to her. As I opened myself to know her better, it made me vulnerable to a host of emotional pulls that I'd never felt for anyone but you. I'm not trying to make my relationship with Evelyn all about her resemblance to my mother, but the similarity did touch an emotional vulnerability that I didn't know existed within me."

He lifted himself up to take another sip of wine and then went back to using her lap as his pillow.

"The more time we spent, the more the impossible started happening; I was feeling love for another woman in addition to you."

"Why didn't you talk to me about it then?"

"I know now that's what I should've done. However, for various reasons at that time, I couldn't bring myself to do that."

"What were those reasons?"

"First, I didn't know why I was feeling what I was feeling about Evelyn to even talk to you about it. I only knew that she began to fill a place inside me. What space it was, I had no clue. My initial effort was to try to resist what I was beginning to feel. I was confident that the man I thought I was had the strength to resist her. However, I didn't realize then, as I said before, there were vulnerabilities within me that were concealed. Again, I'm not trying to excuse away my behavior. I accept all that was wrong with what I did. I'm just trying to explain what I discovered about myself."

"Go on, Solomon."

"Evelyn's resemblance to my mother lowered my defenses and created a curiosity in me regarding her. That curiosity led me to take chances spending time with her, hoping to get to know her better. Doing that put me too far down the track to ever turn back. After I found her within places inside a heart that I thought was only filled with love for you, I didn't know what to do. I was out of my league and could only resort to what men do when they find themselves in those situations: try to conceal it, and that's what I did."

"Why do you think it happened with her and not someone else?"

"I don't know the answer to that question. Her answer was always that it was destiny."

Jan laughed. "Yes, that's her view of life," she mumbled under her breath too low for him to hear.

"What did you just say?"

"Nothing, Solomon. Please continue."

"Trying to cope with the situation tore me apart. I was going to end it, and then things took another turn when I met Jonas."

"What made you think a plural relationship was the answer?"

"I knew there was no answer for you and me—certainly not one that could restore my integrity and keep our relationship intact. I understood I was going to lose you. My actions had put us on that unavoidable course. Therefore, I just had to make a decision for my soul."

"What does that mean?"

"I knew that to restore my integrity as a person, I had to start being honest. Unplanned and unsought, a woman had found her way into my heart, and in the places she came to occupy, I loved her. I had no other choice than to tell you that truth, no matter the price."

He paused for a minute.

"What Jonas and his family did for me was give me the courage and strength to own what I was feeling and to be honest with you and myself. I couldn't turn time back and go back to the place where it was only you in my heart. What I could do, however, was to leave the down-low behavior that I and many other men engage in with women and take another path. Did I think you would say yes to the idea of sharing me with another woman? Absolutely not! But I did want to share with you what I found in Jonas's family: the belief that two women and a man could share a beautiful life together if there was consent and honesty as the foundation."

"Are you still seeking that, Solomon—for you, me, and Evelyn to form a polygamous arrangement?"

"No, I'm not seeking that now. It was simply important for me then to affirm what Jonas and his family affirmed: that polygamy, a valid institution from our African past, remains a real relationship choice. Through Jonas and his family, I'd come to understand its value, particularly for our communities, where plural relationships already exists, but in a way that is destructive."

He continued. "To answer your question, no, I'm not seeking a plural relationship between the three of us now. Since the time I left Chicago, I've only reached out to Evelyn once—to tell her I was going to South Africa and to apologize and encourage her to move on with her life. So much time has passed since then that I'm sure she's with someone else and she's happy."

"What if she hasn't moved on to someone else?"

"I don't know what to say to that, Jan. Evelyn is the type of woman who can easily touch a man's heart. I just can't see her not finding someone else."

"What if she doesn't want anyone but you?"

"Jan, please. Why are you talking like this? You're talking as if you know her or have talked to her. Everything between us is over, and I'm certain she's moved on with her life. I just want to focus on you and me now."

"I'm good with that Solomon. In a strange way, what happened over these past four years made me a stronger woman. There was a lot of pain and anger inside of me from my father's death that needed healing. I tried to bury that pain in my love for you by using you to hide the insecure places inside me that I'd never admitted having to myself, but that didn't work, and I'm thankful it didn't. Because of all that happened, I'm in a much better place now."

"I concur. Looking back over all that happened, I could clearly see my weaknesses, and with them exposed, I had to take the time to make myself whole."

"You remember Kahlil Gibran, that Arab poet you were always quoting to me?"

He smiled. "Indeed I remember."

"You remember the one he wrote on love? Don't you think it aligns with the message we've learned through this ordeal? Just as he said, love will surely take you through some hardships while it proves and tests the strength of your love and prunes your heart to enable you to love more completely."

He smiled again. "Yeah, you're right. It's a perfect poem for what we've been through." Then he began to recite the words from Gibran.

When love beckons to you, follow him, though his ways are hard and steep...

EPILOGUE

The sky turned orange as the sun began to set in Durban. However, there was no need for the sun, as Jan's smile beamed brightly. She was happy that she and Solomon had restored their relationship and were now remarrying.

She held the bouquet in her hand, ready to toss it to a crowd of eagerly waiting women. Most of them she didn't know; still, she was happy they were there to share this moment with her. She looked over at Jonas, Nandi, and Tabisa and moved her lips to say, "Thank you."

Jonas nodded, Nandi smiled, and Tabisa whispered, "We love you."

The crowd of single women grew restless, urging her to make the toss. Solomon reached out, grabbed her hand, and squeezed it as they held each other's gaze.

"Jan, you're a special soul, and I'm indebted to you," he said.

They embraced and kissed once more. Then she tossed the bouquet high over her head. The women scrambled to catch it, with Jonas's sister winning.

Soon the reception was in full swing. After much dancing, everyone settled into relaxation mode. Recognizing that the crowd had tired, the deejay decided to play a slow song to allow for holding and cuddling.

Because he played one of their favorite songs, Solomon extended a hand to Jan, inviting her to the dance floor once more, but she shook her head no.

"My feet won't allow another dance, Solomon, not even a slow one."

Her eyes then urged him to do what she wanted him to do—what she'd asked him to do earlier—even though he was reluctant and uncomfortable carrying out her desire. Nevertheless, she continued to stare at him in a way that insisted he take the actions he was desperately trying to avoid.

Finally, although feeling awkward, he compliantly went over to Evelyn and extended to her an invitation to dance. Evelyn was also somewhat uncomfortable but gladly accepted his offer.

Jan watched as the two of them danced together. First, with much space between them, and then eventually, Evelyn pulled herself close and laid her head on his chest.

As Jan watched them, she thought back to the conversation in which she told Solomon she was inviting Evelyn to their remarriage ceremony. He was shocked. He hadn't known of their interactions over the past two years or of their growing closeness.

She'd told him that without Evelyn her heart wouldn't have healed from the bitterness that enslaved her. He didn't seem to know how to respond to that assertion. He did tell her that he didn't want to do anything to jeopardize his relationship with her a second time, and thus he was uncomfortable with seeing Evelyn and unprepared to be confronted again with her presence. Again, he stated that he'd hoped that Evelyn had moved on and found someone else.

Jan had laughed at that idea.

"Solomon, as much as I hated it when Evelyn said to me that once a woman's heart is open to you, it's impossible for her to move on to someone else, she was right," she'd responded to him. "Evelyn's heart needs healing too, and that healing has to start with the two of you talking to each other again. It's too late for you to simply shut her out and tell her to go and find someone else. You lost that opportunity a long time ago. Now you have to deal with the love that's in her heart for you. What happens to that love is something that must be decided."

She'd come to realize what Evelyn had sensed from the beginning: their three lives were meant to intersect. They'd all lost someone dear to them through tragedies. She and Evelyn had lost the men they loved through war, while Solomon had lost his mother through an accident. Those losses produced feelings that needed tending and mending, and the growing closeness among the three of them was a necessary part of their healing process.

Finding each other was truly no accident. It was, in fact, their destiny.

Yes, that was Evelyn's word. She'd been right all along. Their entanglement was supposed to happen, and their lives had been flowing toward that unexpected end all the time. They'd simply not been aware of that flow, and they hadn't known how to help their journey reach its desired destination.

She continued her gaze as Evelyn held Solomon closely. A few years ago, such a sight would have been too much for her.

My, I've grown a lot emotionally, she proudly admitted to herself.

Moved by the tenderness of their embrace, she put her shoes back on, got up from the table, and walked over to them. She wrapped her arms around Solomon from the back, sandwiching him between her and Evelyn and catching him by surprise.

Evelyn lifted her head up from his chest and smiled at her. Then Solomon pulled her around to his front, and the threesome wrapped their arms around each other and continued to dance together.

The crowd cheered.

The sun had set, but the light of the new moon symbolized that a new and beautiful phase of life was unfolding for the three of them.